She Grew It All Away

By Simon S. Steel

She Grew It All Away

Copyright © 2025 Simon S. Steel

All rights reserved. No part of this book may be reproduced, stored in a retrieval system, or transmitted in any form or by any means, electronic, mechanical, photocopying, recording, or otherwise, without the prior written permission of the author.

This book is a work of memoir. Some names and identifying details have been changed to protect the privacy of individuals.

Printed in the United Kingdom.

First Edition

Cover design by SS

Acknowledgements

To those who never flinched at softness — thank you.

To the wild-hearted women who grew without apology,
and to the men who remembered how to look with
reverence.

To the quiet lovers, the curious minds, the bare bodies in
shared rooms.
To anyone who ever doubted they were enough, exactly
as they were —
this is for you.

And to the friends who never judged the words I wrote
or the worlds I imagined —
you helped make this possible.

Long may we grow.

Prologue

She Grew It All Away

They tell you smoothness is hygiene.
They tell you bare skin is freedom.
But I remember the first time I touched her — and there
was nothing sterile about it.

It was in the back room of a dry-cleaning shop.
No cameras. No implants. No scanners.
Just a flickering bulb and the scent of sweat and citrus
peel.

She wore a slip — nothing more.
She lifted the hem and whispered, *"Not trimmed. Not tamed.
Still want to see?"*
I nodded.

And that was the beginning of it all —
The resistance, the remembering,
The awakening of what had once been sacred but was
now forbidden.

❖ ❖ ❖

Chapter 1
What No One Says

"Clean. Confident. Desired."
The words floated across a thirty-foot billboard above the chemist on Merrin Road.
A woman's body — gleaming, bare, sterile — turned slowly against a background of pastel cream.
Her skin was flawless. Empty, almost.

It didn't offend me.
But it didn't move me either.

She looked nothing like the women I grew up knowing — not in the way their bodies used to *speak*.
Not in the way they felt lived in, complex, textured. Real.

I remember when it was different.
Not long ago in years — but far, far away in meaning.
There was a time when women had hair between their legs and no one mentioned it. No one needed to.
It was just there — like breath, like instinct.

And then, somehow, it wasn't.

I don't remember when the word "pubic" became impolite.
When beauty became bald.
When sex became clinical.
When maturity began to vanish from bodies that were supposed to be ripe with it.

But I do remember before.
And that's where my story begins.

I was thirteen.
Her name was Lucy. She lived three doors down, and her older sister had gone to university, leaving behind a treasure trove of magazines under the bed.

We found them one afternoon — pretending to hunt for batteries.
Glossy pages, creased with time. Models in dim light, backs arched, hands tangled in hair — all kinds of hair.

I remember one photo.
A woman on a velvet sofa, laughing. Legs folded beneath her. No underwear. No shame.
And right there, peeking naturally from between her thighs — a triangle of thick, dark hair.

It was the most erotic thing I'd ever seen.
Because it wasn't presented for effect.
It just was.
Like the warmth of a body. Like truth

I carried that image in my mind for years. Not because it was the first. But because it was whole.
And because it was only the beginning.

There were others, many others —
Bodies soft with confidence, scent rich with desire, hair marking the place where mystery met heat.
From my teens, through my twenties, into my thirties — those encounters shaped me.

Each one different. Each one unforgettable.
Before it all began to fade.

I was seventeen when it happened properly. Not a glance, not a whisper of skin — but closeness. Clumsy, aching closeness that hummed through me for days.

Her name was Tracey.

We'd been in the same year since Year Nine, but only started talking that spring when we got paired for an art project. She smelled of mint and turpentine and wore her hair in loose plaits that made her look older than the rest of us.

It happened on her parents' sofa — corduroy cushions and a flickering lamp left on in the hall. Not much was said. We didn't need to. Everything in our bodies spoke louder than language.

Tracey was calm. Unhurried. And when she leaned back and let me see her fully, I felt the ground shift beneath me.

There was nothing airbrushed about her. She hadn't trimmed or shaped anything.
She hadn't prepared. And she didn't need to.
She was simply herself — natural, warm, utterly confident in the skin she carried.

I remember running my hand gently across her hip, the slight rise of hair that followed her shape, the warmth of it.

I wasn't thinking of what to do next.
I was just there — in awe, quietly burning.

That night changed me.
Because it wasn't just about bodies.
It was about permission. To feel. To explore. To see someone, truly, without expectation or edit.

And it felt like home.

Chapter 2
The Woman Who Didn't Perform

The flat was nothing special — a second-floor sprawl above a launderette, tiles curling at the corners, windows smeared with the ghost of city soot. But that night, everything shimmered.

I remember the warm cling of late summer, the scent of distant rain on concrete, and the unexpected pull of her voice across the room.

"Have we met?" she asked, tilting her head, a half-smile forming at the edge of her wine-dark lips.

Her name was Colette.
I didn't know it then. At that moment, she was simply a woman who knew herself, and that alone was a kind of gravity. She was leaning against the doorframe of a cramped kitchen where the light buzzed slightly, holding a short glass of something amber. A single ring adorned her left hand — not a wedding band, just a thick, dark shape like a smudge of metal poetry.

I was nineteen. Still caught between boyhood and the man I hadn't figured out how to be. My mates had dragged me to the party — if you could call it that. Ten or twelve bodies moving between rooms too small for their need to be seen. Smoke curling out of the half-open window. Someone had spilt beer on the carpet and nobody had noticed. Except her.

"I don't think so," I replied, already sure I'd remember if I had.

Her eyes held mine for a second too long. Not flirtatious. Just... deliberate.

Then she said, "Come here a moment."

She didn't smile as she said it. Didn't blink. She just turned and walked into the hallway, disappearing into shadow as though assuming I would follow.

I did.

Her flat was a short walk away — two roads over, past the glowing mouth of a kebab shop and the drunken cries of someone arguing with their reflection in a bus stop.

She said little.
But the silence wasn't awkward. It felt charged.
Like the whole city had dimmed so we could pass through it unnoticed.

We reached the building — red brick, quiet — and she pressed the buzzer without hesitation. Upstairs, she opened her front door and motioned for me to enter.

The place smelled of bergamot and something woody. Books piled sideways along the floor. A soft, tattered sofa with a cream throw. No television. One lamp in the corner casting honey-coloured light.

She removed her shoes with care, placing them neatly beside the door.
Then she turned to face me and said, "You can sit."

I did, trying not to overthink where to put my hands.

Colette poured two small glasses of red wine, passed me one without comment, and sat opposite me in a straight-backed chair — legs crossed, eyes half-lidded, like this was a rehearsal she'd long since mastered.

"I don't usually do this," I offered, unsure what 'this' was.

She raised an eyebrow. "Neither do I."

Another silence.

Then she stood. "Let's not pretend."

And began to undress.

There was nothing theatrical about it.
No coy glances. No striptease.
She moved as if removing armor after battle —
methodical, elegant, without shame.

Her top came off first. No bra. Breasts full and real, marked faintly by sun and time. She folded her clothes, not tossing them, but laying them over the arm of the chair like sacred items.

Then her trousers. Slowly, steadily, until only her knickers remained. Plain. Cotton. Black.

She paused, and in that moment, looked at me properly — not to check whether I was aroused (I was), but to confirm I was present.

Then, finally, she stepped out of her underwear.

And there it was.

Thick, dark, and impossibly beautiful.
A proud, untouched triangle of pubic hair.

It was the first time I'd seen a woman's body like that —
not edited by porn, not shaved to mimic girlhood, not
concealed or apologetic. Just there. A fact of being. The
centre of herself.

I couldn't move. My erection was immediate, firm,
painful in its urgency.
But what stunned me more was the emotion of it — a
rising tide of reverence, not just lust.

She took one step closer. "You see it."

It wasn't a question.

"Yes," I whispered. My voice barely my own.

"Good," she replied, her voice like silk on glass. "Then
maybe we begin with honesty."

She reached into a drawer and pulled out a long, scarlet
silk scarf.
"Stand up."

I obeyed.

She took my wrists — trembling slightly, though I tried to
hide it — and tied them loosely behind my back. The
knot was soft. Symbolic.
Then she stepped back, studied me, and smiled.

"You're not here to perform," she said. "You're here to
respond."

I sat, bound but unafraid, while she walked around me slowly. Not circling like prey, but inspecting something she had chosen to tend.

She touched my cheek once. Ran a hand through my hair. Let her fingers trail the collar of my shirt.

Then nothing. Just stillness.

The air seemed thick. My breathing shallow.

"I don't need you to impress me," she said, finally. "Just... feel me."

She placed one knee on the chair beside me and let her full, unshaven sex hover close to my face. Not demanding. Just existing.

My senses overloaded.

Her scent was unlike anything I'd known — musky, rich, primal. It was human.
I leaned closer without thinking. She pulled back, gently.

"Not yet," she said. "Not unless I ask."

The restraint made me ache. My erection throbbed, angry and grateful in equal measure.

But this wasn't about pleasure in the way I'd known it. It was something else.
Presence. Ownership. Honesty.

That night, we barely touched in the conventional sense. She kissed me once, deeply. She stroked the inside of my thigh. Once. And then stopped.

She stood naked before me for a long time, letting me take her in.

Then she untied the scarf and said, "Sleep. No sex. Not tonight."

I stayed. She gave me a blanket. We lay side by side in the soft, breath-warmed dark, and I slept like someone who had come home to something lost.

In the years that followed, I searched for women who held that same energy. That *truth*.
But slowly, everything changed.

The women I met were shaved. Waxed. Polished.
It became expected, even assumed.
The term 'Brazilian' became a menu item, not a choice.
Hair became a taboo. A relic. A problem to be solved.

But I remembered Colette.

The woman who didn't perform.
The woman who didn't erase herself.

And in remembering her, I began to realise what had been stolen from all of us.

"It was before Colette — not by much and yet somehow the memory returned only now — perhaps because Colette had awakened something that had been dormant since.

Her name was **Leah**.

She worked in the local library — not the grand, ornate kind with high ceilings and arched windows, but a squat, red-bricked building with flickering overhead lights and the perpetual smell of dust and old glue. I was sixteen. She must have been late twenties, possibly early thirties, though in my adolescent eyes she carried a kind of timelessness — ageless, womanly, and unbothered by the opinions of others.

Leah didn't flirt like Colette. She didn't smirk or lean too close or draw out her vowels. She simply was. Present. Calm. Always in long skirts and soft jumpers, her dark curls half-pinned but always falling loose around her cheekbones. Her eyes had that librarian patience — the kind that suggested she had seen boys like me before, fumbling for confidence, trying to look clever in the philosophy aisle.

But it was never philosophy I was reading when I lingered near her desk.

It happened slowly. A shared glance over the spine of a battered copy of 'On the Road'.

A moment where her hand brushed mine when I passed a returned book. Then a note slipped between pages.

"If you're interested in real stories, I'll be cataloguing in the basement archive at 4."

At first, I thought I'd misread it. But I went anyway.

The basement wasn't locked. It never was. I found her kneeling beside a crate of old returns, her skirt folded beneath her, cardigan sleeves rolled up, fingertips grey with dust.

"I thought you might not come," she said, without looking up.

I said something awkward in reply — I don't remember what — but I remember her smile. It was slow, half-formed, like she knew I had already undressed her in my imagination more than once.

She stood. Brushed the dust from her palms. Walked past me to close the door behind us.

No lock. Just a soft click.

"You're curious," she said. "That's good. But you don't ask questions. That's better."

I could barely breathe.

She stepped closer, and in that moment the air changed. I could smell her — faint soap, something herbal, maybe rosemary or tea tree, and beneath it the warm, unmistakable scent of a woman who didn't scrub herself into sterility. Earthy. Honest.

Leah didn't ask me what I wanted. She took my hand and pressed it lightly against her waist, guiding it down to her hips, holding it there until I steadied. And then, slowly, she leaned in and kissed me — not the hurried, frantic kiss of two teenagers in a stairwell, but slow. Luxurious. Like she was teaching me how.

And in many ways, she was.

She pulled me gently toward one of the archive tables, cleared a few books aside, and climbed onto it — not rushed, not dramatic, just decisive. She wore no underwear beneath the skirt. That I discovered with a mix of shock and awe. She hiked the fabric up without apology, revealing thick thighs, soft skin, and a **dark, lush triangle of hair** that seemed to glisten in the low light.

I'd never seen a woman like that in real life. Not on screens, not in magazines, not in the frantic whispered conversations between boys my age.

She looked like every painting I'd ever half-glanced in a gallery. A nude in profile. A reclining goddess. Real. Whole. Human.

My arousal wasn't a sharp jolt but a swelling heat. It came with reverence, as though touching her was a privilege I hadn't earned.

Leah opened her legs slightly, not wide, just enough — and took my hand again.

"This is how you learn," she whispered, placing my fingers at the edge of her hair, where the heat began. "You pay attention."

I did. I listened. Not just with my ears, but with skin and breath and silence.

The table creaked. Somewhere upstairs, a chair scraped. But we didn't stop. I knelt beside her, unsure of what was allowed, what was wanted — and she guided me, gently, slowly, with just enough touch to suggest, not command.

Her body moved like it had never been taught to be ashamed.

And I learned.

Afterward, she didn't say much. Just kissed me once more and smoothed her skirt.

"You'll remember this," she said.

And I have.

I never saw her naked in daylight. I never took her home, never introduced her to anyone. She was never my girlfriend.

But she was the **first woman** who showed me that sex could be sacred. That a woman's scent, her hair, the warmth of her thighs — all of it could be cherished, not reduced.

Later, when things began to change — when I first heard the word **Brazilian** whispered like a spell in locker rooms and magazines — I thought of Leah.

I thought of how unrepeatable it all felt. How her pubic hair had framed her like a signature — personal, intimate, hers.

And how the world was slowly erasing that signature, one strip at a time.

I didn't know it then, but those two women — Leah with her gentle mystery, and Colette with her blunt, unapologetic hunger — had shown me something I wouldn't come to understand until much later.

That the body, in its natural state, held truths no fashion or grooming trend could erase. That desire wasn't polished or predictable. It was in the soft resistance of untamed hair against my lips, in the scent that clung to skin long after the moment had passed.

And now, years later, when I close my eyes and let the past rise — it's not smoothness or symmetry I remember.

It's them. Whole. Real. Undressed in every sense.

✦ ✦ ✦

Chapter 3
The First Hesitation

I was twenty-two when I met Erin. We were both temping at a small publishing house tucked above a café in Brighton. She wore oversized jumpers, heavy boots, and no make-up — not as a statement, just… because. Erin laughed from her belly, swore in meetings, and once called me an "impossibly well-behaved deviant," which I took as a compliment.

We'd flirted for weeks, folding jokes into editorial meetings and brushing arms in the cramped copy room. When it finally happened, it wasn't dramatic. She leaned on my shoulder during after-work drinks and said, "You can come back to mine, if you're not a twat."

That night, everything moved slowly. Her room was dim and full of plants. The sheets smelled of lavender and something warmer — her, I suppose.

She was confident until we got undressed.

Erin turned her back as she lifted her jumper, then kept her leggings on as she climbed into bed. I joined her, skin against skin, breath heating the narrow space between us.

And still, she hesitated.

I brushed a hand across her hip, waited. When I reached for the waistband of her leggings, she caught my wrist.

"Sorry," she whispered, not looking at me. "I haven't… sorted myself out. You know."

I didn't answer straight away. I didn't quite understand. "Sorted what?"

Her fingers tightened. "Down there. I haven't shaved. It's a mess."

It landed like a language I hadn't heard before. The apology. The shame. As though her body had failed to keep up with some hidden rulebook.

I lifted her chin. "I wasn't expecting you to be anything but human." She half-laughed. "Yeah, well, human's not the fashion anymore."

She let go of my wrist then, slow and uncertain. When I peeled the leggings down, what I found was… beautiful. Coarse in places, soft in others. Dark, slightly unkempt — but completely, utterly her.

And my body responded with the same eager clarity it always had.

We moved together gently. She was quiet at first, unsure. But when I kissed her stomach, then lower — through hair and heat and scent — she exhaled something that wasn't words.

Later, she held my hand in the dark and said, "You didn't even flinch."

I smiled. "Why would I?"

She didn't answer. But her grip tightened slightly.

That night, I didn't sleep. Not because of what we did — but because of what she'd said.

'Sorted out. A mess. Not the fashion anymore'.

It stayed with me, like something shifting in the undercurrent. Not alarming. Just… new.

A few months after Erin, I met Sofia. A sculptor, of all things. Hands like stone and smoke — calloused, strong, delicate in all the ways that mattered. She rented a studio in an old warehouse just outside Shoreditch, and I met her when I wandered in during a local open evening, not expecting anything but free wine and awkward small talk.

She didn't smile when I complimented her work. She just said, "You notice texture."

We ended up back at her studio. The mattress was on the floor, surrounded by half-finished clay torsos, some of them headless, many of them proud and deliberately hairy.

"You sculpt pubic hair?" I asked, more surprised than I should have been.

Sofia shrugged, stripping off her shirt. "It exists, doesn't it?"

There was no performance with her. She undressed like she was alone, not presenting or seducing — simply being. Her body was unapologetic: Mediterranean skin, soft thighs, and the full triangle of dark hair between her legs, thick and slightly matted from the day's heat.

I watched her without speaking. It wasn't lust in that moment — though that came later — it was adoration.

She noticed me watching and raised an eyebrow. "Something wrong?"

"No," I said. "Everything's right."

We had sex on the floor, dust in our knees, sculpture fragments around us. She guided my hands as if shaping me, pulling me into her like I was part of her material world. Every movement, every moan, felt like a reclamation — not just of her body, but of mine, too.

Afterwards, she lay beside me and lit a cigarette.

"I did a piece once," she said, "a whole series of women who stopped shaving because their daughters had started waxing at twelve. One woman told me, 'If we all keep pretending we're smooth, how will the next generation know what real looks like?'"

I didn't respond. But I thought of Erin.

It was around that time I noticed the adverts changing.

On buses. In shop windows. Billboards.

"Feel fresher, cleaner, sexier."
"Be smooth, be confident."
"Because less is more."

Razor brands. Waxing salons. Laser clinics. Bikini models with the word clean stamped beneath them.

Clean.
Confident.
Desired.

It was everywhere. The subliminal message, no longer so subliminal. Hairless was not only the ideal — it was the assumed default.

And anyone outside that default? Outdated. Unhygienic. Undesirable.

I started noticing other things, too.

A few weeks after Sofia, I met Cassie.

She was different.

Clean, sharp, immaculate. From the moment we matched online — one of those early apps where photos were cropped just below the collarbone — I sensed the shift. Everything about her was curated. Not fake exactly, just… designed.

We met in a minimalist bar where every cocktail came with a sprig of something unpronounceable. She arrived in a fitted navy dress, hair sleek, nails precise, not a thread out of place. Even her laugh felt… rehearsed. As if she knew exactly how far to lean in, exactly how long to hold my gaze.

And I fell for it.

There was still warmth there — or the suggestion of it — and I wanted to believe in the kind of woman who seemed to have her life so effortlessly under control.

We went back to her flat, which looked like it had been lifted straight from a design magazine. I remember noticing the absence of anything personal. No photos.

No clutter. Just diffusers, folded throws, and a single abstract canvas on the wall.

We kissed on the sofa. She led me to her bedroom.

And it was there — as she stripped — that something inside me faltered.

Her body was flawless. Sculpted. Hairless from neck to toe. Not just shaved — *treated*. Permanently altered. Even her arms, the tiny down, that would have once shimmered in sunlight, were smooth. The skin between her legs was bare and pink, like it had never known growth at all.

It wasn't revulsion I felt. It was confusion.

Because she was beautiful. Every bit as beautiful as Sofia, or Erin, or Colette before them. But in her nakedness, I felt a strange absence — not of arousal, but of... resonance.

It was like being with someone whose body had forgotten a language mine still remembered.

She didn't notice, or maybe she did and didn't care. We had sex, and she was enthusiastic, skillful, present — and yet afterward, I lay there trying to remember what it felt like to touch her. The memory was smooth, blank, without texture. Like touching marble that had never been clay.

Cassie curled up beside me and said, "I've got my next laser session on Tuesday. You should come with me — they do men now."

I smiled, politely. "Maybe."

But something cracked open that night — something I wouldn't understand until much later.

In the days and weeks that followed, I found myself thinking about Sofia's cigarette. About Colette's sigh. About Erin's breathless whisper. And how all of them — so different — shared one thing in common: they looked like women.

Real women. Adult women. Erotic not in spite of their natural form, but because of it.

Cassie had offered me the modern dream — smooth, flawless, polished. But when I closed my eyes, what I missed was the ache of reality. The slow discovery of warmth through hair. The friction. The scent.

That ache... stayed.

It was maybe two months later, on a cold grey afternoon, when I ran into an old flame at the bookshop on Lever Street.

Rachel.

We hadn't seen each other in years, not since university. She was older now — like me — softer in the face, warmer in the eyes. She wore no make-up, no shapewear, no effort to disguise the living she'd done since we last touched. And I swear, it took my breath away.

We sat for coffee across the road, and for the first time in ages, I felt something I hadn't realised I'd missed.

Ease.

No performance. No script. She didn't fidget with her phone. She didn't mention exfoliation or schedules or Pilates or SPF levels. She talked about her dog. Her mum. A novel she was trying to write. She laughed when she spilled oat milk down her jumper and didn't apologise for it.

I watched the shape of her as we parted. She wasn't airbrushed. She wasn't toned. And yet I remember thinking, 'You are a woman. A real one. And my body knows how to love you'.

That night, I didn't masturbate to Cassie's pristine photos or to any online fantasy. I closed my eyes and remembered the way Rachel once let me kiss her just above the waistband of her jeans — before she laughed, and pushed my head away, whispering, 'Not yet…' in a voice that still had the wildness of young want.

And beneath those jeans, she had hair.

Not sculpted or styled. Just hair. Like a secret kept for me.

And I remembered the feeling of it brushing against my lips like something sacred.

It was subtle. But something had begun to fracture inside me.

Not a rejection of the present — not yet — but a quiet grief for something I hadn't realised was being taken.

Not all at once. Not with banners or warnings. But gradually, by trend and trope. By hashtags and procedures. By the slow reshaping of what we were allowed to desire.

I didn't know then that I was mourning. But I was.

And mourning has a strange way of becoming a kind of prayer.

Even if no one else is listening.

I saw it again on a billboard while walking home.

A sleek woman in a bikini, hip angled, lips parted, body glistening — and not a single trace of hair below her eyebrows. Not even a shadow. Not even a hint that anything once grew there.

It wasn't the image itself that caught me. It was the emptiness of it.

Something about the artificial sheen, the smooth plasticity, pulled me to a stop. I stared a little too long. Not with arousal — but with ache.

It hit me, hard and sudden, the way a scent from childhood might — an old cologne, a specific cut of leather, the sharp breath of cold just before snowfall.

I hadn't thought of **her** in years.

She had laughed when she undressed. Not nervously, not shyly — but as if unbuttoning herself was the most natural act in the world. Her name… yes. It was **Marla**.

She'd been older — not by decades, but enough to know herself.

I had been thirty-ish. Still unsure of my own movements. Still fumbling through the tension between wanting and deserving.

We'd met at a gallery opening in a borrowed suit I didn't fit. She'd worn linen trousers and a low black top, a small tattoo of a swan just under her collarbone. She asked what I saw in a painting and then told me what she saw instead.

That night, I ended up in her flat, high above the station, with windows that looked out over slate rooftops and the slow winking of train signals.

She poured two glasses of something dry and said, without ceremony,

"You're nervous."
I didn't deny it.

And yet — when she undressed, it wasn't with theatre. No lingerie. No ceremony. Just skin and scent and quiet.

She pulled her top over her head, slid her trousers down slowly, and stepped toward me wearing nothing but her body and a slight, knowing smile.

That's when I saw it — full, dark, soft but definite. Her pubic hair, trimmed but generous, curled like an offering.

I didn't realise how much I had missed the sight of it until that very moment. Something ancient and warm stirred in my chest — not just lust, but a kind of recognition. This.

This was what had shaped my early ideas of womanhood. This was what had first awakened the pulse of eroticism in my teenage limbs.

She noticed where my eyes had gone and, smiling gently, reached down and brushed her fingers through it.

"I used to wax," she said, as if casually offering a secret. "Then I stopped. I missed the feeling of being real."

I reached for her, hesitant. She guided my hand. She guided everything.

We didn't rush. It wasn't frantic. She let me explore — not just her curves, but the texture of what was once considered normal. I felt the heat rise in my chest, the pressure in my groin — and the faint embarrassment of being fully, obviously aroused.

But Marla wasn't fazed.

She led me to the bed, lay back with one leg curled at the knee, and watched me.

"Go slow," she whispered. "Let yourself look."

And I did.

I remembered how she tasted — skin salted with sweat and something warmer, muskier. Her thighs opened to me like a promise. I remembered burying my face into the very thing that so many now tried to erase. Her scent. Her hair. Her heat.

She came with a low, beautiful sound, gripping my shoulder, her body tensing and then softening like a sigh that had taken years to release.

We made love twice more before dawn.

When I left, she kissed my cheek and said,

"You'll forget my name, but not this."

She was right.

I had forgotten her number. Her street. Even the exact layout of her flat.

But her body?

The hair. The softness. The way it framed her, held her — made her fully woman and not a sculpted, polished imitation.

That had stayed.

And yet… memory, being what it is, doesn't stay still.

Another image stirred — vivid, lingering.

A redhead. The year or so after Marla. Pale skin, freckles dusted like cinnamon across her chest, and a wild copper tangle of hair that refused to be tamed. She'd had a sharp wit and the sort of eyes that dared you to lie.

But what I remembered most — what had rooted itself in my mind with slow-burning intensity — was the way her pubic hair looked in the low light of her bedroom.

It was the same fiery hue, but deeper. Richer. A burnished amber with hints of gold and rust. It curled thick and natural, like it had never been touched by a razor. It was, to me, intoxicating. Animal and elegant all at once.

As she undressed, the contrast between her pale skin and that vivid, unashamed thatch of red had made my pulse quicken. It felt real. Raw. Like nature itself had insisted on its presence.

I remembered brushing my fingertips over it, the feel of it against my cheek, the way the scent of her was different — earthy, feminine, musky in the way no soap or lotion could replicate.

That encounter wasn't just arousing. It had lodged itself in my erotic memory as *pure*. Not because it was better than others — but because it had felt so unfiltered.

I could still see it clearly. The hue. The warmth of it. The way it glowed in the late afternoon light, catching a beam through the slats of her blinds.

That's what made the shift years later so jarring.

It wasn't just the loss of hair — it was the loss of colour, contrast, and texture.

A palette drained. A terrain flattened.

And though I hadn't known it then, it was the beginning of a kind of quiet grief.

✦ ✦ ✦

Chapter 4
The First Disappearance

It was just a word, spoken lightly, almost playfully, by the woman beside me.

She was leafing through a magazine in bed, legs crossed over mine, sunlight flickering through the blinds across the soft slope of her hip. Her name was Sophie — slender, talkative, with a sharp wit and a habit of finishing my sentences. I'd met her in my early forties, a couple of decades or so after the wildness of Colette, the redhead, and those unfiltered years of sweat and scent and full-bodied hunger.

Now the world felt cleaner. Tidier. Not necessarily better.

"That's the new thing now," Sophie had said, tapping the glossy page. "Brazilian. You can get everything taken off. Well, almost everything — just leave a little strip if you want."

I glanced at the page. A model lay arched in white linen, flawless and smooth, one hand pressed casually across her lower belly. The caption read: 'Confidence is clean'.

It wasn't the image that unsettled me. It was the shift. The assumption. The quiet, surgical language of it — 'everything taken off'.

I remembered lying there, nodding, pretending to understand. But something small recoiled inside me. Not out of prudishness, or nostalgia, but from a sense that something natural — something elemental — was quietly being erased.

That night, while Sophie slept against my shoulder, I remembered another woman. One who hadn't removed a thing.

Her name had been Isla.

She was Irish, though I'd met her in Brighton. Flame-haired, taller than him, with the kind of laughter that warmed a room and the kind of body that made you ache just to be near it.

And yes — her hair down there matched. Not bright, not fiery, but a softer auburn hue. A secret flame.

I remembered the first time she'd undressed for me. The light had caught on every curl, casting soft copper shadows across her thighs. It had stopped me, physically stopped me. She had laughed, not out of shyness, but something older — a knowing. Like she had seen that look before.

"You alright?" she'd teased.

"I wasn't expecting… that," I'd whispered.

"What — that it matched?" she grinned. "Or that it's there at all?"

I'd only nodded, suddenly boyish, and deeply aroused.

I remembered the scent of her. The way she tasted. How the softness of her skin gave way to that textured, untamed warmth between her legs. It had felt alive — not performed, not crafted, but elemental. Like the difference between a wild forest and a trimmed garden.

Isla had let me explore her for what felt like hours. I remembered burying my face into her belly, inhaling the musk of her after a warm day, feeling her thighs tighten, her fingers twist in my hair.

And when she came, her whole body shuddered, like an exhale from the earth itself.

No performance. No scripts.

Just skin, hair, scent, sound — and a rawness I would never forget.

Sophie stirred beside me, a slow stretch beneath the duvet, limbs warm and heavy from sleep. She made a soft sound — part yawn, part sigh — and turned into me, pressing her bare legs against mine. Her skin, still warm from sleep, smelled faintly of almond lotion and cotton sheets.

I didn't move, just watched.

Her hand slid across my chest, fingers curling lightly in the hair there. She opened her eyes, smiled without speaking, and let her fingers drift lower.

I kissed her shoulder. She arched slightly, drawing her thigh over my hip — the duvet slipping, revealing the curve of her stomach and the soft triangle below. Auburn. Natural. Still there.

I paused.

The sight brought a wave of feeling — not just arousal, though that stirred too, quick and familiar. But something else. Something quieter.

A kind of ache.

'How much longer will that be there?'
The thought came uninvited.

Sophie was in her early forties, confident in her body, unbothered by trends. But even she had once joked about "giving in and going smooth" before a summer holiday. I remembered the way she'd said it — breezily, like a passing comment — but the idea had sat in me like a stone.

Now, as her body shifted over mine, as her mouth found my neck, my shoulder, my chest — I responded with instinct, with heat, but also with memory.

Her hands were on me. Her hips moved, slow and seeking. I let it happen, kissed her back, touched her the way she liked — but a part of me wasn't here. Not entirely.

Because behind my eyes, Isla had begun to appear, again.

Another bed. Another time. Another colour, darker — the red of autumn leaves at dusk. Isla had laughed when she caught me staring the first time, said something about the old gods and foxgloves and ginger curses. Then she'd pulled me into her and erased the rest of the world.

I blinked. Sophie moved atop me, breathing harder now.

I closed my eyes and let my body follow, but in my mind, Isla was already waiting.

Sophie moved with me now, slowly, her eyes half-lidded and mouth slightly parted. I was present, yes — in the warmth of her skin, the subtle tension in her thighs, the familiar cadence of her hips. But something in me was split, divided gently between two times, two women.

She leaned forward to kiss me, hair falling around our faces like a curtain. I cupped the back of her head, pulling her closer, but the shape of her hair in that moment — that particular fall of auburn — stirred Isla yet again.

Isla had a way of walking barefoot through her flat, even in winter.
I saw her now — the mismatched socks she refused to wear properly, the chipped red nail polish, the soft humming when she cooked lentils as though she were summoning something sacred.

We met at a small photography exhibition. She was leaning too close to a print of wet moss, lips parted, utterly engrossed. I made some comment about her being more interesting than the art, expecting a roll of the eyes. Instead, she turned, stared at me in complete silence for four seconds, then said, "I'm not interested in being art. I want to be moss."

And just like that — she had me.

Sophie moaned quietly, hips rolling deeper, drawing me back to the room. I opened my eyes. She looked down at me, her expression gentle but focused.

"You alright?" she whispered.

I nodded, kissing her collarbone. "Perfect."

But Isla was still there, behind my eyes. The night we first made love, it was raining hard — the kind of rain that made everything feel distant and secret. Her flat smelled of bergamot and book dust. She was bold. Not aggressive — just assured. When she undressed, she stood in front of me, full and open, red curls vivid against pale skin.

"Don't you dare shave," I had said, almost without thinking.
She'd raised an eyebrow. "You think I do this for you?" Then she grinned, pulled me forward by the shirt, and said, "Though… I'm glad you noticed."

Sophie now tightened around me. Her breath caught. My body responded instinctively — the climax growing in me, steady and urgent. I closed my eyes and let go, feeling her move with me, grounding me.

Afterwards, we lay tangled in silence. Sophie dozed off quickly, her breathing soft and even.

But I remained awake.

In the dim light, I looked at her — her body relaxed, her natural hair soft and still untouched. I was grateful. Truly. But something heavy settled in my chest.

'One by one, they're vanishing'.

It wasn't bitterness. Just a strange mourning. A private, unspoken grief for something so small, yet so defining.

I reached over and gently ran my fingers through the auburn hair between her legs. Just a touch. A simple act of admiration .

Then I lay back and let the memory of Isla carry me the rest of the way into sleep.

It was still raining when I arrived at Isla's flat — the kind of sideways rain that soaked your knees and wrists no matter how tightly you held your coat. She opened the door in a grey t-shirt and no bra, barefoot, her hair pinned messily on top of her head. The flat behind her was dimly lit, golden with table lamps and old bulbs. I stepped inside, dripping and unsure.

"You can leave your shoes there," she said. "And your wet thoughts too."

I laughed awkwardly. "Bit early for that."

She didn't reply — just disappeared into the kitchen, humming.

The place smelled of toasted fennel, jasmine oil, and something earthy. The walls were lined with books, plants trailing down from hooks and brackets. A red velvet armchair was angled oddly toward a corner where a record player sat idle.

I dried my hair with the towel she threw me and watched her make tea. Everything she did had a rhythm, as though her body was conducting a slow jazz track no one else could hear.

When she finally handed me the mug, she sat on the floor, cross-legged, and said nothing for a long time. Just looked at me.

"You always watch people like that?" I asked.

"Only when I'm deciding if I'll let them fuck me."

The tea burned my tongue. She laughed — not unkindly.

That night, I didn't undress her. Isla undressed herself, slowly, with complete ease, her eyes never leaving mine. Her body was pale and curved and entirely hers. She moved like someone who had never doubted herself, not once. She pulled her pants down deliberately and tossed them aside, revealing a soft red triangle of hair between her thighs.

It wasn't neat. It wasn't trimmed. It was wild — full, russet, soft-looking. Something primal shifted in me.

She saw it.

"You like looking at me," she said.

"Yes."

"Say it."

"I like looking at you."

"Say what you like."

"I like your…" I hesitated. "I like your hair. There."

She smirked. "I know."

We made love on the floor first, on a woven rug by the record player. She was strong, unhurried. When I came, it felt like returning to something — not just a climax, but a reconnection. A reminder.

Later, in bed, she curled against me and whispered, "If they ever tell you this isn't beautiful, don't believe them."

I remembered that line more than anything. More than the way she pulled me back in again at 3 a.m. More than the wet sounds and bitten lips and fingernails digging into the small of my back..

'If they ever tell you this isn't beautiful…'

It was a warning, in its way. Or a prophecy.

I never saw Isla again.

Sophie rolled onto her back, drawing the thin sheet over her stomach. Her skin was still warm with the afterglow, breath softening as she turned to me with a lazy smile.

"You're awfully quiet," she murmured, tracing a fingertip across his chest.

I hesitated, eyes drifting downward — not leering, not with lust this time, but something else. The copper-brown patch between her thighs — once wild and confidently

unkept — now shaped, thinned, and softened. Not gone.
But going.

"I was just thinking," I said.

Sophie laughed. "About me, I hope."

"I was thinking about when we first met," I replied. "That
party. You were barefoot. Carrying a bottle of wine with
no corkscrew."

She chuckled. "You opened it with a shoe and a wall. I
thought you were clever."

"I thought you looked like trouble," I said. "The best
kind."

Sophie leaned in and kissed my shoulder. "That night…
was the last time I had it all natural," she added, almost
shyly.

I turned toward her. "Really?"

She nodded. "There was this article… one of those
magazines. Said it made you feel cleaner. More desired. I
don't know… everyone was doing it. It just sort of
became a thing."

"And did it?" I asked. "Make you feel more desired?"

She paused. "I'm not sure. It made me feel... tidier. Neater. Like I was doing something right."

I didn't respond at first.

Then: "It's strange, isn't it? That something so… primal… could become something to manage."

Sophie looked at me. "Does it bother you?"

I shook my head gently. "It's not about bother. It's about noticing. One day it's there — wild, bold, real — and the next it's trimmed, sculpted, smaller."

She smiled, but it faltered. "I never thought about it like that."

"You're not the first," I said softly. "But I remember every first."

Sophie reached under the sheet and found my hand. "Do you want me to grow it out again?"

I kissed her knuckles. "No. I just want you to stay who you are. And for me to remember what was."

I couldn't remember her name.

It was years ago — a hotel room in Leeds, maybe Birmingham. Work trip. Conference. Too many faces and lanyards, too many free pens and sponsored sandwiches.

She'd been a PR consultant, sleek and witty, with expensive perfume and confidence that poured like wine. We'd hit it off over badly poured Prosecco in the lobby bar, laughter dissolving into flirtation, flirtation melting into a cab ride with impatient hands and open thighs.

I remembered her blouse — not removed, just unbuttoned enough — and the way she kicked off her heels with theatrical flair the moment we reached the room.

But most of all, I remembered when she undressed fully, and there was nothing there. Nothing.

Not a single hair.

She had posed deliberately, one knee resting on the edge of the bed, hips tilted, watching me watch her.

"You like?" she asked.

I hesitated, unsure of the right answer. "It's very... smooth."

"That's the point," she grinned. "Sheen is clean, darling. Haven't you heard?"

I had. But not like that. Not with such certainty. Not with pride, or performance.

She crossed the room — naked, polished, perfect — and took my hand, placing it exactly where she wanted me to feel.

"There," she whispered. "No mess. No fuss. Just me. Just skin."

I'd slept with women before who trimmed, shaped, kept things neat. But this was the first time it felt like a statement. A declaration.

She didn't see it as absence. She saw it as upgrade.

Afterwards, I lay beside her, still pulsing with heat, while she checked her lipstick in the mirror, seemingly more concerned with the outline of her pout than any post-coital moment we might share.

I remembered turning on my side, tracing the lines of her hip with a finger, and wondering — for the first time — what was being lost underneath all this smoothness.

Not just hair.

But mystery. Warmth. The quiet, natural invitation of a body allowed to be.

I never saw her again.

But "sheen is clean" stayed with me longer than her name ever could.

I drifted off beside Sophie, her breathing light, the soft curve of her hip brushing against me. But sleep did not bring rest.

In the dream, I was in a vast white bedroom — but not one I recognised. It was too clean. Too empty. There were no clothes strewn about, no signs of life. Just smooth surfaces, crisp linen, and silence.

And then the women came.

One by one, they entered the room. Not real women, not exactly. But echoes — memories, perhaps. Some from youth, some more recent. All beautiful in their own way. All once real. I recognised their eyes, their mouths, their little quirks… until they stepped closer.

Each was bare.

Not just nude — but bare. Down there. Every single one of them. Glossy. Stripped. Unmarked. As though their bodies had been rendered into one silent design. Each time I looked for what I remembered — the soft curls, the natural line, the darkening at the base of their stomach — there was nothing. Just pink. Pale. Polished skin.

They smiled at me. They approached me slowly. Some
knelt. Some opened their legs.

I felt myself stiffen with instinct — but with it came a
wave of sadness, confusion… almost fear.

I tried to speak. To say, You weren't like this.
But my voice made no sound.

They began to whisper.

"Sheen is clean."
"Fresh. Bare. Beautiful."
"All for you. Isn't this what you wanted?"

And then came another voice. Lower. Colder.

"Real women don't look like that anymore."

I looked down at myself. I was fully erect, yes — but also
frozen. Helpless. Unable to move. And when I turned to
the mirror behind the women, I saw myself watching… a
younger version of me. A boy of seventeen, lying between
the legs of my first love, discovering hair, scent, texture
— all of it for the first time. The real thing.

I reached toward the mirror, wanting to climb through it.
To go back. To wake up inside that memory.

But the mirror cracked.

I woke with a start. Heart racing. My mouth dry.

Sophie stirred beside me, still half-asleep. Her leg curled gently over mine.

I touched her hip. Her softness. Her realness.

But a voice remained in the back of his mind.

How much longer will it be there?

The dream had left me unsettled — not in the way nightmares usually do, but with a hollow ache that lingered in my hands. In my mouth.

I turned towards Sophie. Her breath was warm, shallow. Still asleep, or nearly. One arm curled beneath the pillow, the other loosely draped across her stomach. The duvet had slipped just enough to expose the faintest triangle of hair above her centre — darker than the rest of her, soft and untamed.

That sight alone made something stir in me. Something old. Something true.

I moved carefully, pressing a kiss just below her navel. She murmured but didn't wake. I let my hand glide over her thigh, slow and gentle, as if reacquainting myself with something once sacred.

And then I lowered myself.

My mouth found her — softly at first. A kiss. A breath. Then the warmth of my tongue parting her, exploring her with the quiet reverence of a man who had gone too long without knowing if this still existed.

My fingers tangled in her hair — not on her head, but the delicate, fragrant curls that framed her. That welcomed me. That proved she hadn't yet crossed over.

I pressed my face deeper, lips and tongue moving in slow, worshipful circles. The texture of her hair against my mouth, the warmth of her skin, the subtle movements of her body responding in sleep — it filled me with something close to relief. To hunger. To mourning.

She stirred, hips rising instinctively. One hand slid into my hair, not pulling, just resting — anchoring us both in this strange, early-morning half-light.

She whispered my name, not quite awake.

And I thought: 'this… this is what I don't want to forget.'

✦ ✦ ✦

Chapter 5
What No One Says

It had become harder to speak about it — not because it was shameful, but because it had vanished so quietly. No one questioned it. No one talked about what had gone. That slow, deliberate erasure of something once so ordinary, so sensual, so undeniably human.

Pubic hair.

Not in magazines. Not in films. Not in the whispered chatter of men in changing rooms. Not even in the silent glances exchanged after sex. It had disappeared, as if by agreement. As if someone, somewhere, had signed the papers.

I was in my fifties now, and the change was complete. But the memories? They hadn't left me.

I could still see the way it used to be — the deep triangle above the thighs, that first glimpse of dark softness, the way my hands used to tangle in it, my lips parting it as I kissed lower, slower, deeper. The scent, the texture, the warmth — it was all part of the experience. Part of the woman. Not a barrier, not a flaw. A feature.

And yet... somewhere along the line, the world had decided it didn't want women to look like women anymore.

I remembered a girl named Renée.

Not my girlfriend. Not even someone I dated properly. She had stayed over after a long summer evening — too much wine, too much heat, the sound of crickets outside the open window. There had been no pretense between us. She had taken off her dress without ceremony, dropped her knickers beside it, and crawled onto my mattress on the floor.

And there it was.

A thick copper-gold mound, wild and beautifully unkempt. It shimmered in the amber lamplight like something alive. I hadn't expected it — the sight jolted me, aroused me instantly, not just because of how it looked, but because of what it meant. This was not a woman who bowed to trends. She wore her body like truth.

I remembered how I'd kissed her belly first, my hand sliding down, fingers disappearing into softness. She'd moaned, low and relaxed, as if she'd been waiting to be touched like that for years. No one rushed. No one needed to.

That was the difference, I thought now.

Back then, intimacy wasn't a performance. Not everything was curated for viewing — not by others, not even by the person in the moment. There was mystery. There was trust. There was raw, real hunger. And hair was part of it.

I looked around my flat. Sleek lines. Clean surfaces. Nothing out of place.

Much like the bodies now.

But there were other memories, waiting to be recalled.

I closed my eyes.

And another woman rose up from the vaults of my past.

I stayed with Renée a while in my mind.

Not her voice, not her smile, not even the feel of her hands — though all of that had mattered. What remained strongest was the bush. That unmerciful, full triangle of red-gold hair, untamed and defiantly feminine. I hadn't known it would leave such a mark. But even now, decades later, it stirred something deep.

It hadn't been about fetish or fashion. It was biological. Emotional. Animal. The very sight of it had made me feel like a man.

I remembered how it brushed my cheeks when I gave her oral. How it held the scent of her, her taste, her heat. It was a landscape — not a blank, polished surface, but something alive. It tangled in my stubble. It caught my breath.

Later, when she lay on her side, bare leg crossed over the sheet, I had just stared. The way the hair fanned slightly outward, how it formed a soft peak. It had made her look powerful somehow. Ancient. Like something from a time before cameras and razors and silent expectations.

I had seen bushes like that for years afterward. On lovers. in magazines before they became sanitised. And each one told me: 'this is a woman;. Not a mannequin. Not a construct. A living, pulsing, richly-scented human woman.

But they began to vanish.

First subtly. Trimmed. Thinned. Tidy. Then shaped. Styled. Stripped.

Until one day I saw nothing.

Just bare, glossy skin. Like a child's doll. As though the body had been wiped clean of its maturity.

And no one questioned it.

That's what stayed with me more than anything. The silence. The way even women who once wore their hair with pride now spoke of being "clean" only when they were shaved. As if their own natural form was dirty.

I shifted on the sofa. The room was quiet, but inside my chest something swelled — grief, maybe. Or rage. Or just longing.

Not for the women themselves. I had loved some of them, yes. But what I missed was the reality. The resistance. The refusal to perform.

The bush had been more than a patch of hair.

It had been a statement.

And it had been erased.

I'd often wondered about it — truly wondered.

Not in judgement. Not in disgust. But with a puzzled, almost anthropological curiosity.

Why did so many men now seem aroused by something so... empty?

I had tried. Really, I had. There were times when I'd parted a woman's thighs and found nothing there — not a single curl, not a shadow, not even the suggestion of what once was — and I had told himself: 'This is what you're meant to want now'. 'This is desirable. Modern. Sexy.'

But the feeling never landed.

It wasn't about shaming the women. I knew full well that most of them hadn't made the decision for themselves. It was collective. Unspoken. A thousand messages in the air — in magazines, on screens, between the lines of jokes and comments and dating profiles. Smooth. Clean. Bare.

Words that had been twisted until they meant something very different.

But for me, arousal had always been tethered to the real. The raw. The wild. The sight of hair — thick, soft, unruly — spoke of sex, not denial. Of womanhood, not erasure. It said: 'this body belongs to itself.' Not to fashion. Not to the viewer.

Modern arousal, by contrast, felt like theatre. Performance. A sanitised version of lust designed for export.

I would hear other men talk — in changing rooms, on podcasts, even in passing at pubs — and they'd speak with a kind of pride about preferring a bald pussy. As if their preference marked them as refined. As if hair was backward, unsightly, unkempt.

And I'd nod politely. Say nothing.

But inside, something recoiled.

Because to me, the absence of hair had never stirred desire. It had stirred discomfort. A hollowing. A sense that something vital had been removed — not just trimmed away, but uprooted from culture, from language, from the very idea of what made a woman a woman.

I had once tried to articulate it to someone — a friend, long ago. But the words hadn't come right. It had made me sound like a relic, a man clinging to something lost.

Maybe I was.

But I would not pretend to be aroused by what didn't move me.

I would not fake desire.

Not for a fashion trend.

Not for a performance.

Not for a silence pretending to be normal.

It had been sometime in my forties.

She was younger — not by much, but enough for the shift in fashion to show. Confident, sharp, a bit flirtatious.

We'd met through work, bonded over music. I'd found her laugh disarming, her mind bright and quick. For once, the connection had felt fresh. I remembered thinking: 'Don't ruin this with nostalgia.'

We'd kissed in her flat, half-dressed before we even made it to the bedroom. I liked her boldness, the way she reached for me without hesitation. I remembered pressing my lips to her collarbone, sliding her skirt down, my fingers brushing her thighs.

And then... nothing.

No hair.

Not a strand. Not a whisper. Not even a trace of where it might have been.

Just smooth skin. Glossy, bare, like a polished surface waiting to be photographed.

I remembered pausing — not out of judgement, not disgust, just surprise. The sort that you don't know how to hide.

She noticed.

"Don't worry," she'd said lightly. "It's normal. Everyone does it now."

Everyone.

I hadn't said a word. I'd nodded, smiled, kissed her again. But something in my body didn't follow. Not fully.

I went down on her. She was clean, perfumed, well-prepared — and I tried. I gave her pleasure, made her sigh, made her hips lift. But the heat in me — that raw, groaning, ache-in-the-belly heat — never came.

I missed the feel of softness against my lips. Missed the scent that wasn't masked. Missed the wildness.

It wasn't her fault.

She was lovely. Fun. Sexy, even.

But when she fell asleep against my chest, I stared at the ceiling for an hour, wondering what had changed.

Not just in her.

In all of it.

In how a body had become something to be presented, styled, waxed, packaged — rather than inhabited.

I left before morning, quietly, not wanting to explain.

And I never called again.

Not because she wasn't beautiful.

But because she didn't feel like a woman.

Not my kind of woman.

I never told anyone about that night.

Not because it was shameful. Not because she had done anything wrong. But because there wasn't really anything to tell — at least, not in a way people would understand.

What would I say?

That I missed pubic hair?

That a fully bare woman felt unfinished to me, like a statue waiting for its final detail?

I'd tried to explain it once. Over drinks with a friend. The other man had laughed.

"Mate, that's just the way it is now. Clean, confident, desired — that's what women want to be. That's what we're 'supposed' to want."

I'd nodded, played along, even joked back. But inside, something wilted.

It wasn't about being against change. I'd never been afraid of that. It was about what had changed. About what was lost.

It wasn't just hair.

It was mystery. Texture. Identity. The unspoken signal that you were with a woman — not someone polished into submission.

I didn't care about trends or preferences or influencers. I cared about truth. And my truth was simple:

The sight of a natural bush had always made me feel awake. Alive. Wanted. Not as an accessory or a performance — but as a man drawn to something real.

Now, at fifty-three, I sometimes felt like a man with a secret — a longing no one else admitted to. A quiet grief for something the world had shaved away.

It had become a kind of ritual.

When I was alone — truly alone, with no one to perform for, no pretending to be modern or "adaptable" — I'd reach for the old favourites. Not the glossy, fast-cut stuff that filled most of the internet now. Not the endless parade of airbrushed, oiled skin and robotic rhythm.

No.

I needed the 'seventies.'

I needed grainy film, soft lighting, and women who looked like women. Wild-haired, full-bodied, gloriously natural. Women with hips and thighs and thick, dark bushes that framed everything in mystery and warmth.

Sometimes I'd laugh at myself. A man in his fifties scrolling through old VHS transfers and retro erotic reels — as though the modern world had somehow left my libido behind.

But the truth was, I needed it. Without that visual memory, without that familiar image of hair — soft, untamed,…real — arousal came slowly. Sometimes not at all.

It wasn't just what I liked. It was what my body responded to. What my nervous system knew.

No amount of waxed perfection could replace that sense of anticipation — the slow reveal, the parting of curls, the scent of skin as it was meant to be.

These films were more than nostalgia. They were medicine.

Proof that I hadn't imagined it. That once, the world had celebrated exactly what I now missed. And in those dim-lit scenes, I could feel the pulse return. Not just in his body — but in my sense of self.

I remembered waking in the middle of the night — or maybe it was just before dawn. The room still carried the weight of their earlier entanglement, a thick, drowsy warmth in the air. I was on my back, half-covered, the sheets twisted. And there she was.

Straddled lightly above me.

Her thighs were firm but trembling, and the slow, deliberate rhythm of her movements told me this wasn't a dream. She hadn't spoken. Her eyes were closed. One hand at her breast, the other between her legs.

She rocked gently, pleasuring herself, not out of performance — but out of ownership. Comfort. Confidence.

When she noticed I was awake, she smiled faintly, never breaking the rhythm.

"Your turn," she whispered, shifting slightly. "I want to feel what you feel."

And I did. Not from pressure. Not from expectation. But because the moment asked for nothing else. There was no pretending, no posturing — just breath, warmth, and the ancient rhythm of shared want.

She touched me while I touched myself — eyes open, lips parted, like it was the most natural act in the world. It was. Back then.

That night stayed with me — not just because of the sex, but because of how unfiltered it had been. There was hair. Sweat. Laughter. The occasional clumsy elbow or ticklish kiss. But none of it had been curated or waxed away or edited.

It was all there. And I had loved it.

That moment — the night she straddled me in the dark, unashamed and unrushed — opened a vault in my memory. It was like striking a match in a pitch-black attic. Dust lifting. Shadows moving.

There had been others.

Like Eliza, with her thick auburn curls and louder-than-average laugh. She loved to touch herself in front of me. Not for show — but to let me watch what she liked. She'd guide my hand sometimes, or just smile and carry on while I watched, kneeling between her legs like a student at a sacred altar. The way her pubic hair framed every movement made it feel ceremonial — primal, even. It focused the eye, anchored the act.

Then there was Danica. Bold. Sharp-minded. Older than me. She didn't believe in hiding anything. She'd lie back on the rug, draw my hand down, and say, "Don't be delicate. Be deliberate."

She taught me the power of rhythm. Of pressure. Of silence between breaths. Her pubic hair was dark, almost black, and coarse — and she liked when I ran my fingers through it as a kind of foreplay. She said it reminded her that she was real. Not some vision, not a doll.

"I want to feel like a woman," she once said, guiding me between her thighs. "Not a billboard."

And I had felt it. Every moment with her had pulsed with intention. Mutual pleasure wasn't just encouraged — it was expected. Welcomed. She gave as much as she took, always meeting my eyes when she slid her hand between my legs, as if to say: 'This is mine too'.

The memories came in waves now. Different women. Different nights. Same grounding presence. The bush. The scent. The untrimmed, undiluted truth of desire.

That's what it had meant to me — not just visual appeal, but texture, character, honesty. You couldn't fake it. You couldn't sculpt it into a fashion.

Back then, it was just part of her — like her laugh, her scent, her voice.

Now, I thought, it had become a silence. An absence.

Like something erased without permission.

✦ ✦ ✦

Chapter 6
The Spark in Real Time

It was a small local gig — nothing remarkable, just a moody basement bar with live guitar, a dusty stage, and a familiar ache of bass that rattled through the concrete floor. I hadn't planned to go, but my friend Ella had dragged me out, as she often did when I'd been too quiet for too long.

"Just music and a drink," she'd said, knowing I wouldn't need more than that.

Ella had been my friend for years. Sharp-tongued, leather-jacketed, and effortlessly cool. She made no apologies about being gay — or about still having her pubic hair.

"Why the hell would I shave for anyone?" she'd once said, laughing into her pint. "If a woman can't handle my bush, she can't handle me."

I'd always liked that about her — not just the honesty, but the ease she carried it with.

The bar was humming now. I stood near the back, sipping something dark and bitter, when Ella nudged me with her elbow.

"See her?" she said, tilting her head subtly toward the bar.

I followed her gaze. There she was. Tallish, curly-haired, wearing something sheer over a tight black vest. Her smile was warm but unreadable. Her name — as we later discovered — was Nia.

We talked. The three of us. Nothing flirty at first — just stories about bands, terrible first dates, the state of coffee in small towns.

Then Nia turned to me, brushing a strand of hair from her cheek, and said, "I like the way you look at people when they talk. Like you're listening to more than just words."

I felt the warmth behind her eyes. And Ella must've sensed it too.

Later, out in the smoking area though none of us smoked, the conversation shifted.

Nia was bisexual. Had dated men and women. Had been single for about six months.

"Do you have a type?" Ella asked her.

"Not really," Nia replied. "I like people who make me feel more like myself."

There was a pause, the kind that hums with possibility.

Then — bold as ever — Ella grinned and said, "OK but let's get shallow for a second. Are you smooth? Shaven?"

Nia blinked, then laughed. "Nope. I've got a bush. A big one."

She said it like a challenge. Or a dare. Not defensive — just certain.

Something lit up inside me. I hadn't expected it. Not here. Not like this.

But the heat rose up my chest and curled around my ribs. She had a bush. She still had one.

I swallowed.

"Good," I said softly, without thinking.

Nia turned to me, slightly amused. "Good?"

I shrugged, feeling the pulse in my neck. "It's... rare these days."

Ella raised an eyebrow but didn't interrupt. She knew me well enough to let it unfold.

Nia's voice dropped to a velvet softness. "Would you like to see it sometime?"

And in that moment — bass trembling through the walls, the scent of rain on brick, Ella's knowing smile half-caught in the corner of my eye — everything slowed.

"Yes," I said. "Yes, I really would."

Ella's flat was above a record shop, tucked between an old printmakers and a florist that only opened Thursdays to Sundays. The stairs creaked. The light in the hallway flickered. But inside, it was soft and golden, strung with fairy lights, velvet throws, and incense that smelled faintly of orange peel and something herbal.

"Shoes off," Ella said, toeing hers into a basket by the door.

Nia wandered in with a quiet curiosity, trailing her fingers along the spines of records stacked in shallow crates. "Feels like a den," she murmured.

"It is," Ella grinned, "and the rules are simple. No judgments, no rushing, and always — always — more cushions than necessary."

We settled in with wine — an open bottle from last week that still tasted fine. Music played low from an old speaker. Something jazzy and slow. There were no sudden moves, no forced flirtation. Just the hum of something rising.

Nia curled her feet beneath her on the floor cushions. She looked at me differently now. Less guarded. More curious.

I hadn't felt this kind of heat in years. Not the brash kind that surged and spilled — but the quiet one, the coiling warmth of knowing, 'this could actually happen.'

I sipped slowly.

"I meant what I said earlier," Nia said suddenly. "About the bush."

I looked up.

"I've never liked the idea of removing it. I don't know... it felt like erasing something. Like pretending I'm not grown."

Ella laughed gently. "Preach."

I nodded, setting down my glass. "It's more than just appearance," I said. "It's a kind of... energy."

Nia tilted her head. "Energy?"

"Yeah," I said. "Texture. Scent. Wildness. It's what made things feel adult. When I was younger, I couldn't get enough of it — the look, the feel... the way it framed a woman's body. Now it's rare. Too rare."

There was silence. A respectful kind.

Then Nia shifted closer. "Do you want to see mine?"

Ella raised an eyebrow, but stayed quiet.

My breath hitched, not from nerves — from hunger.

"Yes," I said.

Without standing, Nia leaned back slightly and undid the zip at the side of her skirt. It slid down her thighs like falling silk. She wore no knickers.

And there it was.

Thick, soft, full. A dark auburn mound, untamed but clean. Framing her like a secret she didn't apologise for.

I stared. Reverent. Quietly undone.

"Touch?" she asked.

I reached. Fingers trembling not from fear — from devotion.

The first stroke was gentle. I combed slowly through the hair, feeling the warmth beneath it, the way it cushioned and invited.

It was real.
Alive.

She sighed, not from arousal yet, but from being *seen*.

Ella moved then, coming to sit beside Nia. She didn't interfere. Just rested her hand on Nia's thigh. "God, I've missed this," she murmured. 'A man who understands.'

I looked up at her. "I've been remembering it all my life."

And then, Nia leaned in and kissed me.

Not hurried. Not hungry.

Just real.

We moved to the bedroom together. No one rushed.

Ella lit two low candles on the windowsill. One flickered against the bookshelf, the other drew shadows across the folds of the bedspread. The room smelled faintly of sandalwood and skin.

Nia stood beside the bed, still half-dressed, her auburn hair loose down her back. Her skirt already gone. Her blouse now open. Her full bush catching the candlelight like something sacred.

I undressed slowly. They watched me, not with hunger, but warmth — curiosity, even admiration. It had been years since I'd felt naked and wanted, without performance.

"Lie down," Nia said softly.

I obeyed.

She straddled me — just above my hips — and let her fingers trail down my chest, pausing at my stomach, then tracing her own navel. I couldn't look anywhere but down.

That thick, natural mound hovered above me. Framed in shadow. Framed in memory. But this was no memory.

She leaned forward, letting it brush my chest. I inhaled deeply, the scent unmistakeable: musky, human, arousing in a way nothing polished or waxed had ever been.

Ella settled to the side, one hand beneath her chin, just watching.

"I want you to taste me," Nia said.

I didn't need asking twice.

She shifted forward, her knees either side of my head. Lowered herself slowly.

And there it was — her full bush brushing my lips, soft and coarse all at once, curling at the edges and slightly damp with anticipation.

I opened my mouth and breathed her in.

Every lick was a return. Every press of my tongue to her clit was a defiance against a world that had tried to erase this. I wrapped my hands around her thighs, pulled her down further. She gasped, hips shifting, hair brushing my cheeks. I felt it around my lips, against my nose, exactly as I remembered from long ago.

Ella moved closer, her hand now stroking the inside of Nia's leg, helping her stay steady.

Nia was trembling — not from climax, not yet — but from being worshipped. Fully. Truthfully. No edits. No airbrushing.

I licked deeper. Slower. Letting my nose press into her mound. Letting her hair tangle with my breath.

She moaned. "I've never… been eaten like this."

I smiled against her. "Then they didn't know how to love a woman."

Ella reached for my hand. Guided it to herself. She was soaked. I stroked her as I licked Nia, and suddenly there were three bodies in rhythm. Unrushed. Unguarded.

The night unfolded in rhythms — first Ella, then me, then both together. The woman's laughter, the way she held us close, the scent of sweat and skin and something ancient.

Later, when the three of us lay tangled in the heat of the sheets, limbs lazy and entwined, I stared at the ceiling with the softest grin on my face.

Nia turned to me, her voice sleepy and satisfied. "You okay?"

I nodded. "I think I just travelled twenty years back."

Ella chuckled. "Good trip?"

I closed my eyes, feeling the weight of Nia's hair on my chest, the warmth of her still-damp pubic mound resting against my hip.

"Best trip I've taken in years."

And for the first time in a very, very long while, I felt… whole.

Chapter 7

The Summer House

It was a borrowed cottage near the coast — a half-crumbling summer house belonging to someone's aunt who was "away indefinitely." I had been twenty-four. The woman I was seeing at the time, Justine, was a gallery assistant who smoked clove cigarettes and painted her nails black before it became fashionable. She knew everyone. Or at least, everyone interesting.

That weekend, it was just the two of us to begin with. I remembered salt air through open windows, the stick of cold cider bottles, the scratchy sofa in the sitting room. But mostly I remembered the heat Justine brought with her. She had the kind of body that always felt like it had just been in the sun — warm, loose, unapologetic.

And then there was Leigh.

She arrived late on the second night, hair wind-blown, lips stained red from something they'd been drinking in the pub down the lane. She and Justine greeted like sisters. Not family — but bonded. There was a long-held secret between them.

I didn't ask what it was.

That night, they lit a fire and drank too much. Leigh sat cross-legged in front of the hearth, her dress hanging off one shoulder, revealing just a trace of downy red hair under her arm. Justine, barefoot, draped across the armchair, met my eyes once or twice with a knowing smile.

It happened with no plan.

Leigh was the first to stand. She stretched, yawned, and said, "I need to cool off," then pulled her dress over her head with no ceremony at all. She wore nothing underneath.

The sight took my breath — the bold, natural way she carried her body. Between her thighs, there was no trimming, no shaping — just a proud, flaming triangle that seemed to glow in the firelight.

Justine didn't blink. She reached for my hand. "Come on then," she whispered, "don't look so shocked.

We spent the night on a mattress dragged to the floor. Sheets loose. Candles burning low. Leigh's voice was deeper than Justine's — slower, more instructive. At times she took the lead; at others, she simply watched, eyes half-closed, her hand curled behind Justine's neck or sliding gently between my legs.

It wasn't chaotic. It was... orchestrated. Like a jazz piece. Improvised. Intimate.

I remembered the sensation of lips on my chest while fingers raked gently through my hair. I remembered burying my face into the space between Justine's thighs while Leigh stroked her hand slowly down my spine.

I remembered, most of all, how completely I had disappeared into it. The scent. The heat. The hair.

It was there — on every woman I loved — like a soft
frame for everything I desired.

Now, lying beside Ella and the woman from last night,
our bodies still warm from sleep, I thought back to the
summer house — the smell of salt and cider and old
books, the hum of bodies, and the freedom of that one,
long, moonlit weekend.

I exhaled, slowly.

'Some things really weren't better in the past', I thought.
'But some things were.'

✦ ✦ ✦

Chapter 8
The Secret Club

It started as a joke, really.

The three of us sat in Ella's kitchen the next morning, still half-naked under loose dressing gowns, sipping strong coffee from chipped mugs. Nia sat cross-legged on the countertop, her hair wild, her bush even wilder, grinning as she recounted how many men had told her to shave.

"'It's cleaner,'" she mimicked, rolling her eyes. "'More hygienic.' Honestly, it's like they think I'm walking around with a compost heap between my legs."

Ella snorted into her coffee. "If only they knew what they were missing."

I leaned back, smiling lazily. "We should start something," I said, half-serious. "An appreciation society. The League of the Bush."

Ella raised an eyebrow. "The League?"

"No, better," Nia said, hopping off the counter. "Make it sound a bit sexy. Mysterious. Like those old jazz clubs with passwords and curtains."

I chuckled. "The Velvet Root?"

We laughed for a good minute. But then the silence came — not awkward, but loaded. As though all three of us had simultaneously realised... why not?

Ella turned serious. "Actually... maybe we should."

I looked at her. "You mean it?"

"Think about it," Nia said. "Everyone's so curated now. Trimmed, waxed, filtered. There's nothing *real* anymore. And I know I'm not the only one who's had enough of it."

"We could start small," Ella said, leaning forward. "Private invitations. A few friends who 'get it.' Keep it discreet."

"Safe," added Nia. "Non-performative. Just... natural. Erotic in a grown-up way."

My heart thudded. It felt like something had cracked open — not just in us, but in the world. A quiet rebellion. One muffled moan at a time.

That evening, we began planning.

A name. A symbol. A phrase that meant something only to those who remembered the scent of skin in winter, the softness of curls against lips, the first time they felt hair under their tongue and knew — this was sex, this was woman, this was real.

And so *The Wild Follicle Society* was born.

"Right," Ella said, pulling a notepad from the kitchen drawer like it was a boardroom meeting. "First rule: no phones."

"No digital trail," I nodded. "No photos. No profiles. Just word of mouth."

Nia twirled a spoon lazily. "You realise this sounds like we're starting a cult."

"We *are*, in a way," Ella grinned. "A cult of curl."

I nearly choked on my coffee.

We all leaned in now, the mood shifting from playful to conspiratorial.

"What would a new member have to do?" Nia asked.

"Vouching system," said Ella. "No random invites. Every guest has to be brought in by someone who's already been."

"And confirmed," I added. "As in, confirmed to carry the bush or to genuinely crave it."

Nia tapped her mug. "But not performatively. It's not about trends or fetish. It's about real erotic return. The restoration of… of texture."

We all paused. That word. Texture.

"Yes," said Ella softly. "We're bringing back texture."

I smiled. "And how do we keep it secret? Do we use a location each time?"

"I think we do it in private homes to start," Nia suggested. "Rotating. Keep it intimate. No more than… twelve people."

"Twelve's good," Ella nodded. "Twelve's symbolic."

I looked up. "Passcodes?"

Nia's eyes lit up. "Yes. Silly ones. Or clever ones. Or just plain filthy. Like… 'Velvet in the Valley.'"

Ella snorted. "Or 'The landing strip is closed.'"

I laughed, then said, with mock gravity, "*The fox is in the hedgerow.*"

We were hysterical for a good minute.

Eventually, Ella wrote them all down.

Proposed passphrases:

- *The fox is in the hedgerow.*

- *Velvet in the Valley.*

- *No blades, no shame.*

- *Curly returns.*

- *Friction is fiction.*

- *Woollen welcome mat.*

- *We honour the halo.*

- *Slick is a trick.*

"We'll choose one each time," Ella said. "Something you whisper through the door before we let you in."

"And," I added, "members are welcome in any state. Fully grown, lightly trimmed, even if they're regrowing. No judgement. Only intention matters."

Nia raised her mug. "To the intention."

We clinked mugs.

Then Ella said, "But we need a symbol."

I paused. "Like a pin? Or a card?"

"No," said Nia. "Something subtle. Like a scent. A handmade oil. Something that lingers."

"A scent…" Ella's eyes lit up. "What if each gathering has its own oil blend? A ritual. A shared scent for that night's memory."

"And made with natural ingredients only," said Nia. "Something sensual. Earthy. Slightly musky."

I smiled slowly. "We're really doing this."

Ella nodded. "Oh yes. And it begins next Friday."

The kitchen was bright with late morning sun, and the three of us sat around the table — bare legs tangled, mugs half-full, toast untouched.

Ella had one of her sketch pads open, jotting ideas as fast as they came.

"Not *The Wild Follicle Society*," she said, underlining it twice. "Too jokey. We're not joking."

Still shirtless, I stretched and looked over her shoulder. "We've already said it.'

The Hedgerow."

Nia, hair a mess and lips still pink from kissing both of us, took a long sip of black coffee. "Sounds secret. Slightly forbidden. I like it."

I smiled. "It should feel like something people whisper about in dark corners."

Ella nodded. "So… underground gatherings? Erotica nights? Story sharing?"

"Live readings," said Nia, "but only of bush-themed encounters. No shame. No pretending it's a phase or a punchline."

I leaned forward, eyes alive. "We can have a *Hedgerow Tales* evening — everyone brings a story. Anonymous entries get read aloud."

"And no one judges," Ella added. "You either love the bush, or you're learning to love it."

We all laughed.

Nia reached for the pen, flicking through the pad to a blank page. "What about initiation?"

Ella grinned. "Ah yes. There has to be a rite of passage."

I raised an eyebrow. "You're not going to suggest… visual inspection?"

Nia smirked. "Of course not. But maybe a little challenge. Like… bringing your first bush story. One that meant something. Could be real, could be fantasy."

Ella tapped her lip. "And a passphrase to enter."

In thought I said. "What about… 'Thick as truth'?"

Nia blinked. "That's… actually quite beautiful."

Ella scribbled it down with a flourish. "Done. The first *Hedgerow passphrase.*"

We paused for a moment, caught in the hush that follows a decision that feels real.

Then Nia said, "I want to go first. My story. One I've never told."

Me and Ella sat back, listening.

Nia set down her mug. "There was this girl, early twenties. She was Italian. I met her on a language exchange. I thought she was straight, and I was wrong."

Ella smirked. "Always a pleasant surprise."

"She invited me to the lakes. We went swimming. She stripped off without a word and dove in. When she came back out, standing on the rocks, water streaming down... it was the first time I'd ever seen a bush like that. Dark. Full. Wild. It was… beautiful!. That's the word."

My eyes softened. "It changes you, doesn't it? That first time."

Nia nodded. "Yes. Because it wasn't for anyone. Not styled. Not 'maintained'. It was just... her. Free."

Ella looked down, quiet now. "I've got one."

I turned to her.

She cleared her throat. "Back when I still thought I was straight, I dated this guy. We were young. He'd never gone down on anyone before. And the first time, he told me I smelled like warm moss. Like something he wanted to get lost in."

Nia blinked. "That's poetry."

Ella smiled. "He didn't know it, but he was the first to make me feel like I never had to remove a thing."

I tapped the table. "I've got mine too. But I'll save it for the next story night. Let's write the rules first."

"The only rule," Nia said, "is honesty."

"And desire," Ella added.

"And," I said, "that a bush is never up for debate."

The Hedgerow had begun.

Nia glanced at the clock above the stove. "Shit. My cat's going to murder me."

Ella grinned. "He's probably halfway through your curtains by now."

Nia stood, stretching her arms above her head with a soft groan. "Thanks for last night, both of you. I haven't felt that seen—or satisfied—in years."

I smiled, genuinely. "Same here."

She slipped on her jacket, kissed us both on the cheek — lingering just slightly longer with Ella — and whispered, "Don't let this fizzle. We've started something."

And with that, she was gone, the front door clicking shut behind her.

The flat fell quiet again. Only the soft hum of the kettle and a faint birdsong outside.

Ella leaned back in her chair, twisting a loose strand of hair between her fingers. I looked at her, really looked. Without the haze of last night or the brainstorming energy of this morning. Just the quiet pull of something unspoken.

She tilted her head. "You've got that look."

I raised an eyebrow. "What look?"

"That 'I'm about to kiss you without a word' look."

I didn't say anything. Just stood, walked around the table, and kissed her.

No fanfare. No tension. Just warmth. Familiar, natural.

Ella reached up under my shirt, her hands flat against my chest. "We don't have time to start anything proper," she whispered against my mouth.

"Doesn't have to be proper," I murmured, lifting her effortlessly onto the kitchen counter.

Her legs wrapped around my waist instinctively. A giggle escaped her throat — half surprise, half need.

"I'm not wearing anything under this," she whispered, tugging her oversized T-shirt up slightly.

"Good," I said simply.

It was fast. Urgent. Like scratching an itch that had waited too long.

No slow undressing, no dramatic build-up — just the sound of breath, a tug of fabric, and the press of skin on skin. The kind of quickie that didn't need to prove anything. No performance. Just connection.

Ella's hand gripped the back of my neck, teeth catching on my shoulder as I moved inside her.

When it was over, we stayed there for a moment — bodies still touching, heads pressed together, both catching our breath.

Then she smiled. "Okay. Now 'that's' how you end a meeting."

I laughed, pressing a final kiss to her lips before stepping back and dripping on my thighs .

She jumped down, adjusting her shirt, still grinning. "See you soon, Hedgerow man."

I gave her a wink. "Sooner than you think."

Chapter 9
Laughter in the Quiet

I closed my front door and leaned against it, keys still in my hand. The silence of my flat wrapped around me like a familiar coat — the hum of the fridge, the soft creak of floorboards, the faint tick of the wall clock.

I stood there for a moment, eyes closed, and let out a breath I didn't realise I'd been holding.

Then I chuckled.

It started low in my chest — more of a release than a laugh — but it quickly bloomed into something fuller, warmer, more bewildered.

I set my keys on the counter and wandered to the sofa, falling back into the cushions like a man who had just survived something extraordinary. Or perhaps entered something extraordinary.

I rubbed my face with both hands, still grinning. "What the hell just happened?"

Nia — goddess of a woman with a mane that turned me to liquid. That bush — bold, magnificent. And Ella — my lesbian best mate, my confidante, the one person I never imagined I'd end up in bed with. Let alone after sharing a woman together.

And then there was *The Hedgerow* — the name that had started as a cheeky in-joke over coffee and toast and now pulsed with the strange, wonderful possibility of something... real.

I couldn't stop smiling.

I ran a hand through my hair, still slightly mussed from the morning's unplanned pleasure. It all felt absurd. And yet, it was the most me I'd felt in years.

I reached for the small notebook on my coffee table — the one I usually used for shopping lists and scattered thoughts — and flipped it open to a fresh page. At the top, I wrote in bold, underlined capitals:

THE HEDGEROW

Beneath it, I scrawled ideas as they tumbled from my head:

- *Invite-only gatherings*
- *Anonymous stories — read aloud in candlelight*
- *"Bush and Brush" life drawing sessions*
- *Symbol: a spiral hidden in foliage?*
- *A velvet pouch with a handwritten passphrase*
- *Perhaps... a scent? Something earthy, musky — a perfume of memory*

I paused, tapping the pen against my lip.

Who wouldn't want to be part of something like that?

I laughed again. Not the ironic kind. Not bitter. Just… joy. That curious, ticklish joy of something just beginning.

I looked around the room. Same furniture. Same walls. The smell of sexual pleasure.

'I need a shower' With that. I knew something had shifted.

The Hedgerow had taken root.

The flat was still.

Ella stood barefoot by the sink, hands wrapped around a chipped mug of coffee. The morning light fell through the blinds in soft strips, dust hanging gently in the beams. Somewhere in the street below, a delivery van idled, a dog barked once, and then — silence again.

She leaned against the counter, the warmth of the mug anchoring her as her mind played back every beat of the night before.

Nia. That glorious creature. The confidence, the ease, the full, magnificent bush that made Ella's thighs tense with longing the moment it was revealed. She could still smell her — that deep, animal musk, earthy and sweet and maddening.

And then Simon.

Bloody Simon.

Her best friend, the man who used to read her break-up texts aloud in funny voices to make her laugh, the one she always thought of as a bit hopeless but loyal to the core. And now? She'd seen him differently. Not in theory — in practice. His tongue between Nia's thighs. His hand brushing hers mid-way through. That flash of surprise when she'd reached for him too. And that moment, later, between just the two of them. Unexpected. Unspoken. Natural.

She sipped her coffee and licked her lips slowly.

No regret. Not even confusion.

Just... yes.

The Hedgerow.

The name still made her grin. It had begun as a laugh — half-ridiculous, half-brilliant — but now it felt like something alive. Something raw and ready and needed. A rebellion. A remembering. A way to reclaim desire that didn't come waxed and bleached and hollowed out.

She reached for the notebook they'd scribbled in that very morning. Still open on the table, ink smudged at the corners. Her own handwriting alongside Simon's and Nia's:

"Not a society. Not a club. A **cove**."
"Where stories are the entry." "Where hair is not removed but revered."
"Where no one needs to apologise for scent or softness or depth."

Ella ran her fingers over the page, then closed her eyes. She could still hear Nia's laugh — low, rich — and Simon's breathless 'what are we doing?" as they stood tangled in the half-light.

She smiled to herself.

They were doing exactly what they were meant to.

The cat was furious.

Nia could hear him the moment she reached the stairwell — that impatient, throaty yowl that always greeted her when she was late home. But instead of rushing up, she paused halfway, resting her palm against the cool metal banister.

She needed a moment. Just one more breath before stepping back into normal life. Because nothing about last night had been normal.

She started walking again. Her thighs ached slightly — deliciously — and her body still hummed. She felt like she'd been dipped in something golden. Not just from the sex — although that had been superb — but from the honesty of it. The joy. The way no one had hesitated when she unzipped her skirt and let the wildness of herself show.

She opened her front door, fed the cat, poured some water into a chipped ceramic bowl, then slumped down onto the old sofa in the bay window.

Nia wasn't the kind to get sentimental about flings. But last night didn't feel like a fling.

It felt like the beginning of something else.

Not a relationship. Not a threesome turned awkward. But something older. Richer. A feeling she hadn't had in years. Maybe not since her early twenties, when a girlfriend had first whispered in the dark, 'Don't ever shave, Nia. That's your power."

Back then, it had been a quiet rebellion. A refusal. Now, though? Now it felt like a *calling*.

She pulled her phone from her coat pocket. Two new messages from Ella.

"Still can't believe last night. We have to do this."
"Simon's already texting me names. 'Velvet Grove' is his current favourite, but I told him 'The Hedgerow' is unbeatable."

Nia laughed out loud, softly so as not to startle the cat.

The Hedgerow.

She liked it. She liked that it sounded like something you had to push through. Wild, tangled, secret. Not manicured. Not easy.

She stood and walked to her dresser. Opened the drawer where she kept things she didn't usually wear — silk, lace, the kind of knickers that spoke in whispers rather than giggles.

She took out a pair. Soft plum-coloured. Vintage French.

She didn't know why, but she slipped them on.

Something was coming. She didn't know what. But she could feel it.

And this time, she would be ready.

Nia stood beneath the hot water, hands pressed against the tiled wall, the spray cascading over her hair, her shoulders, her breasts.

The night still lingered in her body.

But now, it wasn't lust that buzzed through her veins. It was purpose.

She closed her eyes.

Simon's fingers. Ella's kiss. The laughter. The taste. The scent of something real, something natural, reclaiming space in a world that had become flat, hairless, polished to sterility.

'We're not meant to be smooth. We're meant to be wild.'

She whispered the words to herself, letting the steam seal them into her skin.

After the shower, she wrapped herself in a towel and padded barefoot into the lounge. The cat was curled up, finally content. The flat smelled faintly of lavender.

She dried off, dressed, and made a coffee before settling at the small dining table with her phone.

Call One: Jess.

Her oldest friend, a tattooist with no filter and no shame. Nia didn't launch straight into it. She talked about the gig. The wine. The wild night. And then, quite naturally, she said:

"We're starting something. A movement, maybe. It's not just about sex, but it's also very much about sex."

Jess laughed, then swore, then said she was in.

Call Two: Maree.

A bi woman from her old book club who once said, in passing, "I only date women who let themselves be women." Nia hadn't forgotten.

Maree didn't laugh.

She paused and said quietly, "I've been waiting for something like this."

Nia hung up, heart beating a little faster.

She opened her laptop. The screen stared back — blank, expectant.

She typed:

The Hedgerow Manifesto (Draft)

We are the ones who remember.

We are not ashamed of what grows.

The Hedgerow is not a place — it is a principle.

Our pleasure is not manufactured.

Our bodies are not edited.

The hair we keep is not a trend.

It is a protest. A celebration. A remembering.

She sat back, fingers tingling.

It was only a start — a seed. But seeds, when planted, could root deep.

She reached for her notepad next and scribbled:

- *Meeting spaces*

- *Erotic storytelling nights*

- *Secret garden theme?*

- *Velvet invite cards — old-school, wax-sealed*

- *A whispered phrase at the door…*

She smiled.

It wasn't just about pleasure.

It was about returning to something no one dared say aloud anymore.

Hair. Sex. Power. Nature.

The Hedgerow was waking.

I shut the bathroom door with my heel, dropped my towel to the floor, and let out a low, incredulous laugh.

The kind of laugh you let slip when no one else is around. A laugh that says, What the hell just happened?, and just grinned.

Nia.
Ella.
The sound of laughter echoing in a kitchen full of candles and kink.
The feel of fingers not meant to be there, being *exactly* there.

And the bush — dear God — the bush. Like something I hadn't just missed, but mourned. Until last night.

I walked barefoot to the sofa and sat, topless, hair a mess. I didn't even bother to make tea.

My phone buzzed.

Nia: *"Still grinning? I am. And planning. Brace yourself, Simon. The Hedgerow is real."*

I stared at the message, thumbs hovering.

Simon: *"You're serious?"*

She replied instantly.

Nia: *"Deadly. Ella's in. I've already made two calls. We're growing something here. And I want you at the centre of it."*

I sat up.

Me?

I was never at the centre of things. Not movements. Not meaning. Just quiet observations, memories tucked into old boxes of magazines, and the occasional wistful search for seventies erotica that didn't come airbrushed and childishly bare.

But now...

Now something had been uncovered. Literally.

I opened a drawer and pulled out one of those old magazines — the kind I'd kept all these years, more out of defiance than nostalgia.

I flipped it open.

A centre-fold of curls. Of woman. Of heat.

Back then, it was normal.

Now? It was revolution.

The phone buzzed again.

Ella: *"I still can't believe last night happened. But also — yes, it did. I want more. I want this."*

I closed my eyes and let the images flicker behind my lids — the curve of Ella's thigh, Nia's lips, the scent of real, grown, mature sex. Not polished. Not preened. Not prepackaged.

I took a deep breath and typed one reply — to both of them:

"Then let's begin.

"I didn't yet know what The Hedgerow would become.

But it felt like purpose.
It felt like pleasure.
It felt like coming home.

I stood at the bus stop, barely aware of the passing cars. My mind wasn't on the route or the destination — it was on her. The one from the café yesterday. Casual, natural, quietly beautiful. She'd laughed at a joke her friend told, leaned forward slightly… and there, just at the edge of her jeans — the unmistakable curl of something real.

It had made me dizzy. Not with lust — that came later — but with *hope*. She didn't seem like someone who would show up to an underground gathering called *The Hedgerow*. But maybe, just maybe, she was someone who felt it too. That private unease with the way everything had been stripped smooth, sanitised, glossed.

I decided to try something.

Not seduction. Not persuasion. Just… conversation.

That evening, I went back to the same café. Not to stalk — I'd been clear with myself on that — but just to see. She was there again, sitting with the same friend, this time with her hair tied up and a paperback in hand.

I approached the counter, ordered tea, and took the table near the window, angled just enough to catch the light chatter of her table.

Minutes passed.

Then, a moment — her friend left to take a call.

I turned slightly, offering a polite smile. "That's a rare sight these days," I said, nodding at her book. "Most people just scroll."

She looked up, a little surprised, then returned the smile. "I like paper," she said. "You can't swipe it away."

Our chat was gentle at first. Books, music, the noise of the city.

Then she asked, "Do you live round here?"

I paused, then decided to try honesty. "Sort of. But I've been… building something lately. With a couple of friends. It's a bit odd. A bit niche."

Her brow arched with interest. "Odd is good. What kind of thing?"

I hesitated, then said it.

"It's called *The Hedgerow*. It's… a kind of movement. Well, more like a conversation. About how certain things — natural things — got erased over time. Especially for women. And how maybe, not everyone was okay with that."

She tilted her head. "You mean body hair."

I nodded.

She didn't laugh.

Instead, she looked thoughtful. "You know… I don't really talk about this stuff with anyone. But I stopped shaving two years ago. I got tired of feeling like I was supposed to be twelve."

I felt a warmth in my chest.

Maybe, I thought, the women I was hoping to reach didn't need converting. They were already there. Just waiting for someone to say it's okay.

✦ ✦ ✦

Chapter 10

Simon's Way

I stepped into the bakery on a rainy Tuesday afternoon, more for the warmth than the bread. The bell above the door gave a gentle chime as I entered, brushing drizzle from my coat. It was a small place, homely — wooden shelves, handwritten chalkboard, the smell of flour and butter in the air.

Behind the counter stood a woman I hadn't seen before. Late thirties, perhaps. Curvy, soft-featured, hair tied loosely in a bun. No makeup. No airs.

I smiled. "This place smells too good to pass by."

She returned the smile — not flirty, just human. "Well, you're just in time for the almond pastries. Still warm."

I ordered one, made some small talk. The usual: weather, queues, prices. But I watched her. Not like a lech — just curious. A small tuft of hair peeked just above the collar of her blouse. Natural. Untouched.

I took a risk.

"Odd question," I said, breaking off a piece of pastry, "do you think everything needs to be trimmed to be appealing these days?"

She looked up, caught off guard, but not offended.

I softened it with a grin. "I mean in general. Beards, hedges, habits… people seem obsessed with making things tidy."

There was a pause. A flicker behind her eyes.

She leaned in slightly and said, "Some things are better left wild. Depends who's looking, doesn't it?"

I felt something shift. Just a little.

Not a seduction. Not yet a lead.

But maybe — maybe — a doorway.

Scene: Seeds in the Wild

I didn't follow the bakery woman on social media. I didn't ask her name, or leave my number. That wasn't the point.

I'd learned something from that short exchange — about tone, curiosity, permission. Not every conversation needed a goal. Some just needed to land, like a pebble dropped in a pond.

Over the next few days, I tried again. Not with speeches. Not with leaflets.

With moments.

At a garden centre, I asked the cashier — a young woman with dyed green hair and hands dusty from compost — whether wildflower patches were making a comeback. She grinned and said, "They never left. People just got obsessed with control."

A conversation about moss in driveways turned gently into one about body image. About permission. About softness. I didn't steer — I let her talk.

At a bus stop, an older woman in her fifties complimented my coat. We laughed about how everything used to be made better — warmer, thicker, more real. I nodded, and simply said, "And not just coats, either." She looked at me, held my gaze for a beat too long, then smiled without reply.

Each encounter was different. No names exchanged. No invitations. But they stayed with me.

I began carrying a small notepad in my coat pocket — not to write down names, but moments. Words that stuck. Expressions. Little reactions. Not for analysis. Just to remember how it felt to connect with the wild, the real.

Back at my flat, I added to a growing list of possible themes for *The Hedgerow* gatherings:

- ***The Shape of Memory***
- ***Permission Without Performance***
- ***The Body Before Filters***
- ***Textures We Forgot***
- ***Bush as Rebellion***

It wasn't a campaign. It was a restoration.

And I knew, somehow, the movement would grow not through noise — but through resonance.

Scene: The Antique Lamp

I didn't go out looking for it.

I'd wandered into the shop on instinct — one of those bric-a-brac places tucked between a dry cleaner's and a closed-up café. The smell of wax polish and forgotten stories.

She was rearranging lampshades. Long brown hair tied up, dark roots showing. Older than the green-haired girl at the garden centre. Maybe late thirties, maybe more. Bare arms, lightly freckled. Real. Uncurated.

I asked about the Tiffany-style lamp in the window.

"That one's not for sale," she said, brushing hair from her cheek. "Was my mum's. But I've got similar ones inside."

We spoke for around fifteen minutes. About light. Warmth. Texture. The way modern LED bulbs flattened everything. I told her — simply, gently — that I liked things with a bit of weight to them. A bit of shadow.

Her name was Bridget. She didn't flirt. But she didn't move away either.

I offered to buy her a drink. She said yes, but only if they made it two. She needed loosening, she said, after days of "polite, airless conversations."

It was later that night, back at her place — not planned, not chased — that it happened.

I was slow, respectful, sensing I could ruin it with the wrong kind of eagerness.

But when she pulled her dress over her head, there it was. Her pubic hair — thick, full, dark, soft-looking — like a defiant answer to everything I'd quietly mourned.

I didn't speak. I just looked. Gently touched. Kissed the top of her thigh. Then lower.

She closed her eyes and whispered, "I don't get many who actually… want this."

I smiled against her, brushing my cheek into her warmth. "I do," I said. "God, I do."

There was no performance between us. No pretense. Just skin and warmth and quiet, breathless rhythm. I gave, and she gave back. Not as a show, but as a shared remembering.

Afterwards, lying together with fingers tangled, she said, "You didn't push. You didn't sell anything. You just… listened."

I nodded.

"It's a good method," she murmured.

I kissed her temple.
"It's not a method," I said softly. "It's just remembering what matters."

The Kitchen Confession

Nia arrived just after eight, clutching a brown paper bag of pastries and a bottle of something fizzy. Ella raised an eyebrow.

"It's Tuesday morning," she said, gesturing at the bottle.

"Exactly," Nia grinned. "Tuesday is the most forgettable day of the week. I say we make it memorable."

They sat by the window with mugs of coffee, nibbling pastries and scribbling on napkins and scraps of paper. Ideas spilled easily now: themes, anonymous submissions, meet-ups in candlelit garden rooms, vintage erotic readings, a zine perhaps. Every suggestion brought a new thread, a new excitement. *The Hedgerow* wasn't just a joke anymore. It was breathing, forming.

Somewhere between laughs and lists, the bottle was opened.

By late morning, the fizz was gone, and the room was full of warmth. Not just the sun pouring in through the net curtain, but the warmth of shared secrets and slowly blooming want. Nia sat cross-legged on the floor, her fingers playing with the hem of Ella's loose shirt. Ella stood, leaned against the kitchen counter, cheeks flushed with a grin that lingered too long.

"I've not done this," Ella murmured.

"Done what?" Nia looked up.

"This. Liked a friend."

Nia tilted her head. "You didn't like me that night?"

"That was want. This is… something else."

A pause.

Then Nia got up. Moved close. "I'm alright with either," she whispered. "But I need to kiss you again."

Ella didn't answer. She just let it happen.

Their mouths met softly, then hungrily. The kiss deepened as Ella's hands found Nia's waist, slipping beneath the soft cotton of her top. There was no rush, just a quiet knowing. Like two plants growing toward the same light.

Nia's hands unbuttoned Ella's shirt one by one, exposing her slowly — not just the skin, but the person beneath. She kissed her collarbone, her breasts, then dropped to her knees, lifting the hem of Ella's oversized grandad shirt with admiration .

There was no surprise between them — only relief that the want was mutual.

Ella laid back on the kitchen table, chest rising and falling, hair mussed, skin glowing. Nia keeling between Ella's thighs, teasing at her clit and tracing small circles on her hip.

"This is the Hedgerow," Nia whispered.

Ella nodded. "And it's only just begun."

✦ ✦ ✦

Chapter 11

Rooted & Rising

I had made tea, but no one was drinking it.

Nia had brought wine again — "for the muse," she claimed — and Ella was already cross-legged on the floor, scrawling potential slogans onto a sheet of recycled parcel paper. The flat smelled faintly of toast, lavender oil, and mischief.

"The Hedgerow," she repeated aloud, letting the word roll across her tongue. "I still love it. It's earthy. Secret. Slightly rude if you know where to look."

Nia chuckled, curled up on the sofa in one of my oversized jumpers. "We're the first resistance movement to grow out of someone's knickers."

Leaning on the kitchen counter, I smiled. "You say that like it's a bad thing."

I stepped forward, holding out a second sheet of paper. "I jotted these earlier. What d'you think?"

What was never meant to vanish
No shame. No blades. Just roots.
Come as you are — truly.

Ella clapped, delighting in the phrasing. "That one — the last one — that's a winner."

Nia poured another round. "So, are we actually doing this? A logo? A patch? A—what? Bush-shaped enamel pins?"

I looked down into my wine and paused.

"There's something else," I said, quieter now. "Someone else, actually."

Both women turned to me.

"I met someone. Bridget. And… it wasn't just about the sex — though we had that too. It was the moment she undressed, and there it was — a thick, proud, utterly unashamed bush. I couldn't stop staring. Not in a gawping way. Just—grateful. Relieved, almost."

Ella tilted her head. "Like confirmation?"

I nodded. "Exactly. It wasn't just you two. It wasn't a fluke or some rare relic. She chose it. She maintained it. She understood it. And I felt…" I paused, searching for the word, "safe. Like the Hedgerow already exists — in secret, in women like her."

Nia smiled. "Then we're not starting something new. We're rejoining something ancient."

Scene: Bridget Joins the Hedgerow

I wasn't sure what Bridget would make of the Hedgerow. She'd seemed curious when I'd first explained it over wine and candlelight — half amused, half intrigued. But now, sitting across from me in the pub garden, she looked more thoughtful than playful.

"You weren't joking about that name, were you?" she said, sipping her drink. "The Hedgerow. It's mad. But it's kind of... brilliant."

I smiled. "It started as a laugh. Now it's... turning into something real."

Bridget leaned forward. "So what is it, exactly? A movement? A fetish club? A bush appreciation society?"

I shook my head. "It's not a kink thing. Not really. It's about something older. About how the world's been trimming women down to fit a script — to look younger, cleaner, more controlled. The Hedgerow is about unlearning that. It's messy, warm, real."

Bridget tilted her head, watching me. "You sound like you've thought about this for a long time."

"I have," I admitted. "But it's only now, with Nia and Ella — and now you — that it's starting to feel like more than a memory."

She was quiet for a moment. Then: "You know... I've got friends. Three, maybe four, off the top of my head. All hairy. All quietly proud of it. They'd love this."

I raised an eyebrow. "You're serious?"

Bridget nodded. "Deadly. And not just for the sex. Though — that's obviously part of it," she added with a grin. "But it's more... I dunno. Comforting. Empowering, even. I've hidden under clothes at beaches. Shaved for jobs, dates, expectations. But left to my own devices? I grow. It's who I am."

I felt a quiet warmth rise through my chest.

Bridget leaned in. "So if there's a next meeting, I want in. And I'll bring company."

Scene: The First New Faces

It was a Friday night, and my flat was glowing with low amber light and the faint scent of bergamot and red wine. Nia and Ella were already there, spread comfortably on cushions, flicking through scribbled ideas in the Hedgerow notebook. Slogans, sketches, stories. Laughter. Wine.

Then came the knock.

Bridget entered with a calm smile and two figures behind her — a woman with long, wild brown hair and a relaxed presence, and a man in his forties, lean and thoughtful, wearing a threadbare jumper and a nervous smile.

"This," Bridget announced, "is Lara and Tom. And before anyone panics — yes, they both know what this is. And yes, they're in."

I stood slowly, nodding to Lara first. She stepped forward, confident but open. "I think what you're doing here is… overdue. Hair has always been part of who I am. And lately, I've missed having anyone to talk to about that."

She turned slightly. "Tom, though — he's the surprise."

Tom gave a soft laugh, eyes lowered at first. "I didn't think I'd ever speak this out loud. Not in a room like this.

But Bridget told me about the Hedgerow, and for the first time in years I didn't feel… odd."

I crossed my arms, still unsure. "And what is it you're looking for, Tom? Be honest."

Tom met my gaze. "A place to say that I miss what women used to be allowed to be. I miss softness. Wildness. Hair. I don't want shaved precision. I want warmth. Fragrance. I want to run my hands through something real — not pretend it's a relic."

There was a quiet pause. Nia raised an eyebrow, watching my face carefully.

I sat down, finally. "Alright. You're not alone."

Tom exhaled slowly, relief spreading in his shoulders.

Lara looked around. "So… when's the next gathering?"

Bridget smirked. "I think we're already in it."

Scene: Tom's Story

They'd all settled now — cushions pulled into a loose circle in my lounge, glasses refilled, a plate of olives half-forgotten between us. The notebook lay closed beside Ella's thigh. No more scribbling tonight.

Just stories.

I glanced at Tom. "You said you missed something. Something that used to feel real. Start there."

Tom nodded. Not nervous now — just steady.

"I was twenty-three. She was called Lizzie. Wild hair, wild opinions. She rolled her own cigarettes and never wore a bra. Said bras were 'compliance stitched in cotton.'" A soft smile crossed his lips. "She was the first woman I ever went down on. And the first to tell me, in the gentlest way, that I had no idea what I was doing."

A few chuckles. Even I cracked a grin.

"But she taught me. Showed me what to feel for. And god… there was so much. The scent, the softness, the warmth. Her hair framed it all. It wasn't decoration — it was invitation.

I remember one moment, just… burying my face into her. Hair brushing my cheeks. Her thighs tightening. I was lost in it. Like being in a field that had grown wild and free."

He paused, eyes distant.

"And I loved that. Loved being swallowed up. Loved that it wasn't neat or bare or cold. She smelled like sex and skin and earth. I remember thinking — this is what it means to *be* with someone."

He took a breath. "But then… the world changed."

I leaned forward slightly.

"I remember sleeping with someone about ten years ago — I think her name was Kara — and she was waxed smooth. Nothing. Not a single hair. She told me it was 'what men preferred.' I didn't say anything at the time, but I missed it. And it kept happening. Woman after woman — bare, bare, bare."

Tom looked at me now. "I didn't speak up. Not once. Until Bridget told me about this." He gestured at the others. "I thought maybe I was just behind the times. That something primal in me was simply... obsolete."

My gaze was unreadable, but deep down, something had shifted.

Tom swallowed. "But I want to feel *that* again. That wildness. That sense of... not everything being filtered, controlled, groomed into submission. I don't want The Hedgerow to be a gimmick. I want it to be a return."

Silence followed. A full, honest silence.

And then — I nodded.

"You're in."

Scene: Nia's First Time with a Woman

The air had softened again. No one rushed. They sipped slowly, eyes warm with wine and trust.

Nia sat cross-legged, her arm draped loosely over the back of my chair, her fingers playing with the rim of her glass. She looked over at Ella. Then Bridget. Then to Tom and Me.

"I was twenty. Had just come out of a terrible relationship with a man who called pubic hair 'lazy'," she said with a dry smirk. "He used to flinch if even one hair poked out of my knickers. I started waxing just to shut him up."

She shook her head gently. "Then came Jess."

I noticed the slight change in her voice — it was softer now. Not hesitant. Just fond.

"She was in my uni seminar group. Studied photography. Always had a camera round her neck and this way of laughing like she didn't care who heard her." Nia smiled at the memory. "One night, we stayed behind after a gallery visit. Everyone else had gone home.

We wandered the halls. Talked about everything and nothing. Eventually she asked if she could take my photo."

The room held its breath a little.

"It wasn't a line. It wasn't flirty. Just pure… curiosity. Art. I said yes. We ended up back at her place. She pulled out this old film camera, set up a little corner with soft light, and asked me to strip."

Bridget raised her eyebrows, impressed.

"I didn't feel exposed," Nia went on. "I felt seen. Every time she clicked the shutter, it felt like something was being reclaimed. She told me I looked beautiful with hair. That it suited me. That it was me."

A pause.

"Afterwards, she put the camera down. And kissed me."

I felt something tighten and release in my chest.

"It was gentle at first. But sure. Like she'd been thinking about it long before I had. I'd never touched another woman. I didn't know what I was doing. But I remember thinking — this is why I never liked how men touched me. They were always skipping past the good parts."

A few quiet laughs.

"We made love slowly. Her fingers in my hair. Her mouth on my skin. Her face between my thighs. She took her time. And when I did the same to her, I finally understood what it meant to be worshipped — and to give that worship back."

She met each of our eyes in turn.

"She kept her hair natural too. Full, auburn, soft as moss. That's when I knew — I wasn't just bi. I was alive when someone loved themselves fully. No shame. No hiding."

Tom looked stunned. Ella looked radiant.

I simply nodded. Deep, quiet gratitude.

Lara's Turn

Lara rested her hands around her mug, the heat seeping into her palms as she glanced between all of us. The flat was warm, dimly lit, with a faint hum of music playing from my speaker.

"I've been quiet," she said, her voice calm but purposeful. "Because for me… this isn't just fun or curiosity. It's something I've carried."

Ella turned to her gently, and Nia leaned in.

Lara continued, "I'm straight. I've only ever been with men. And I can tell you, for the last fifteen years, I've been made to feel like something's wrong with me… simply because I never wanted to change what was natural."

She paused. "I used to feel beautiful — honestly. Like that part of me meant something. But more than one partner made me feel embarrassed for it. Said it was unclean. Outdated. Like I was 'too much.'"

I looked down, brows knitted.

"I don't want to be told again that the real me is 'too much,'" Lara said, lifting her head. "That being natural is somehow unattractive. I want to feel… allowed again. Wanted. Seen."

A hush fell over the room — not awkward, just tender.

"I didn't come here expecting anything. But listening to all of you — it's reminded me of something I thought I'd lost. A kind of quiet pride. I'd like to be part of this, if you'll have me."

Bridget gave a soft smile and raised her glass. "Welcome to The Hedgerow."

And just like that, Lara felt… home.

Ella's Turn

Ella had been lounging cross-legged on my sofa, her half-empty wine glass balanced on one knee. When Lara finished speaking, she reached forward, set the glass down on the coffee table, and gave a quiet sigh.

"I've got one," she said, brushing her fringe out of her eyes. "It's not dramatic. But it's… mine."

We all looked up, giving her their attention without interruption.

"I was fifteen when I realised I liked girls," she said, with a small smile. "It wasn't some big awakening. It was Jade Wheeler in the school changing rooms. She had this gorgeous dark hair — all the way down, you know? Curled around her thighs like something out of a forest fairytale. And I remember thinking… that's what a woman looks like."

She laughed softly, not embarrassed. "I didn't even know I fancied her until I saw that. It wasn't just desire. It was awe. Like I'd stumbled on something sacred."

Nia nodded slowly, lips parted slightly, and Bridget gave a warm hum of agreement.

"And when I started dating — girls and boys — I noticed something," Ella went on. "Girls were starting to shave everything. Boys were starting to expect it. Suddenly, it wasn't beautiful anymore. It was shameful. Something to be erased."

She looked at me, then to Lara. "I tried it once. Took everything off. Looked in the mirror and didn't recognise myself. Felt like I'd vanished — like I'd tried to mimic something smaller, younger… less me."

There was a short silence.

"So I stopped. And over time, the lovers changed too. I found the ones who liked *me* — the full, messy, powerful version. I remember one night — I'd just started seeing this girl, Tash — and she buried her face in me and said, 'God, you smell like *you*. Don't ever change that.'"

Ella's voice softened to a whisper. "And that was the moment I knew I'd never go back."

She reached for her wine again but didn't drink. "That's why I'm here. That's why *The Hedgerow* matters. Because no one should feel erased just for growing as they were meant to."

Bridget clinked her glass to Ella's without a word.

I smiled, quietly grateful. This wasn't just rebellion. This was reclamation.

Simon's Story – The First Touch

I had been quiet while the others shared. Not out of shyness, but because my story lived further back — in a place few people asked about anymore.

I glanced down at the rim of my mug, then spoke.

"I was... well, very young," I said, eyes still lowered. "Old enough to know what I was doing, but too young to realise how much it would shape me."

The group leaned in, silent.

"We were at someone's house — one of those teenage gatherings where the adults are away and nobody's sure what the rules are. I ended up alone with her on a battered armchair, half-lit by the glow of a hallway lamp."

"I remember the nerves, the fumbling. But I also remember what I felt. My hand moved — hers guided it — and there it was."

I looked up.

"Hair. Warm, natural, inviting. Not something out of a film or a magazine. Something real. And for me, something unforgettable."

I paused, and in that moment, it wasn't a memory — it was a truth returning to the room.

"I didn't know it then, but that moment would stay with me for the rest of my life. It wasn't just about sex. It was about something that said: this is a woman."

I looked around.

"And ever since, I've never stopped searching for that feeling again — until now. Until The Hedgerow."

✦ ✦ ✦

Chapter 12

A Different Kind of Bloom

Ella hadn't expected it to change her. Not like this.

She stood by her bedroom window, tea in hand, hair still damp from the shower. The morning light made everything soft — the curtains, the floorboards, the curves of her bare shoulders beneath the cotton of her oversized shirt.

It had been days since that night, but it kept replaying. The gig. Nia. The way Simon had looked at her — not with confusion or caution, but hunger. Real, aching, physical hunger. For her.

And it had lit something she hadn't felt in years.

Not just desire, but recognition. Like her body had been waiting, quietly, for permission to return to the world. As if the act of being desired by a man again — a man she trusted — unlocked something long sealed.

She hadn't stopped thinking about it since. About Nia's laugh. Simon's mouth. The taste of skin. The feel of the bush — hers, theirs, the celebration of it.

It made her wet just remembering. And it wasn't just arousal. It was power. Permission. A quiet reclaiming of something that had been politely trimmed away over the years.

She sipped her tea and smiled.

She was blossoming into something else. Not a different woman exactly. Just... more of herself.

And The Hedgerow — that ridiculous, brilliant name they'd thrown around in the kitchen — it had already taken root in her.

Maybe it was just a gathering. Maybe it was a movement.

Maybe it was both.

Ella set the mug down on the sill and pulled the curtains just enough to soften the daylight. The loose cotton of her shirt brushed the tops of her thighs as she walked back to the bed, and she suddenly became aware of her body again — the warmth between her legs, the way her nipples pressed lightly through the fabric.

She sat.

She hadn't done this in ages. Not like this. Not slowly. Not with memory.

But it wasn't just any memory. It was the feeling of Simon's hands on her waist. The heat of Nia's mouth. The soft press of three bodies tangled in laughter and scent and hair.

She let her palm rest against her thigh.

God, that moment — Nia, peeling off her skirt without shame, the glorious curl of her bush exposed and proud. Simon watching, breath caught. Ella herself, surprised by how much she wanted to bury her face in that wildness. And how she had.

Her fingers moved gently, trailing along her skin.

She parted her legs.

This wasn't about fantasy. This was remembering what had already happened. Her fingers found the damp warmth gathering there, and she let her head fall back as the rhythm began.

She thought of Simon again — how surprised he'd been that night. How his tongue had lingered on her lips. How it hadn't felt like some big dramatic turn, just… natural. Easy. Right.

Then Nia, kneeling between them, reaching out, stroking both of them at once like she was painting something sacred.

Ella's breath hitched.

And her own bush — the one she'd kept for years, quietly, half out of habit — was now a source of pride. Of joy. Her fingers moved more firmly now, curling inward, the pressure building.

She moaned softly.

It wasn't just lust. It was a reclaiming. Every stroke reminded her: she was allowed this. Hair, hunger, heat — all of it.

When the orgasm came, it was steady. Deep. It rippled through her with no apologies.

Ella lay back, one hand between her legs, the other curled over her breast. The morning light kissed her skin.

She was different now.

And *The Hedgerow* was blooming.

I sat by the window with my coffee going cold. The morning after glow had worn off, replaced by something far less easy to name. He looked around the flat — the cushions still messy from last night's gathering, a half-full glass of wine left on the bookshelf, a lone black bra slung over the back of the chair.

The Hedgerow.

What had begun as a laugh — a playful phrase tossed between the three of us — was now shaping into something with roots. Intent. Desire. But whose desire?

I rubbed my jaw, still sore from Lara's thighs. That memory — God, what a night — came with a pulse of arousal that faded quickly into something like guilt. Or was it just doubt?

Was this really a movement? A reclamation? Or had he accidentally created a space that conveniently let him act on every pubic-hair-fuelled fantasy he'd suppressed for decades?

Ella. Nia. Bridget. Now even Lara Tom.

It wasn't that they weren't sincere. They were. And they each had their stories, their reasons, their longing for naturalness — for honesty. But still…

Was I secretly building a soft-lit harem disguised as resistance?

I looked down at my phone. A message from Ella: *"Still can't stop smiling. We've really started something, haven't we?"*

Then one from Bridget: *"I've spoken to two more friends already. They want to meet us."*

My gut twisted. Was this what leadership felt like? Or was it manipulation under another name?

I needed clarity. Not another orgasm. Not another night of limbs and laughter and hair curling between fingers. I needed to know whether this was just a kink with a manifesto — or something bigger, braver, real.

I stood and began to tidy. Not the usual lazy shuffle. Proper tidying. Grounding. Sorting cushions, folding throws, stacking mugs.

As I gathered Nia's scarf from the floor, a few long auburn hairs caught on the fabric, catching the morning light. I paused.

Not just lust.

But not purity either.

Just truth.

I folded the scarf gently and whispered to the quiet flat, "Let's find out what this really is."

I didn't text her. I just turned up.

Ella opened the door in joggers and a messy bun, surprised but not annoyed. She stepped aside to let me in without asking why I was there — because she already knew.

She handed me tea without milk, sat across from me on the floor cushions, and waited.

I took a sip, then looked at her — really looked. Not with lust, not with performance. Just presence.

"I feel like I've done something wrong," I said, finally. "And I don't even know what it is."

Ella didn't blink. "Because you started The Hedgerow?"

"Because I started something that feels… convenient. For me. I keep replaying it. All of it. That night, last night, Nia, Bridget, Lara,…..you, the ideas, the stories. And it's like — am I building a movement, or did I just find a clever way to sleep with women who still have pubic hair?"

A pause. Ella studied me. Then exhaled — not with frustration, but something closer to relief.

"Simon," she said, gently. "You didn't manipulate any of us. I'm not here because you seduced me into a cult. I'm here because I want to be. Because it's real — the loss, the shame, the way things have shifted. I feel it too."

I swallowed. "But is it just a fetish? Is it perversion dressed up as purpose?"

"No," she said firmly. "Fetishes live in secret. This isn't secret. This is reclamation. It's not about what turns you on — it's about why it turns you on. Why it used to be normal. Why it isn't now. And how something so small — hair — became a battleground."

She leaned forward, touched my knee. "You're not making this up. You're remembering what felt good before it got erased. There's nothing wrong with desire. Especially not when it's rooted in honesty."

I let out a breath I didn't realise I'd been holding.

Ella smiled. "You're not the only one building this. It's not yours alone."

I nodded. "Still feels… weird."

"It should feel weird. We've all been conditioned to think we're strange for wanting what's real. But it's not strange. It's just us — remembering."

There was a long silence. Comfortable.

Then I said, "You're very wise for a lesbian."

She grinned. "You're very emotional for a straight man."

I laughed — properly laughed. And that was the moment I felt it: the guilt loosened, the knot inside slowly unwinding.

Not perversion.

Not performance.

Just two friends, and a truth worth telling.

◆ ◆ ◆

Chapter 13
The Line Must Be Drawn

Bridget had a glow about her the next time she turned up at my flat — the unofficial Hedgerow HQ. She swept in with two people in tow: a softly spoken woman named **Kate**, and a tall man with slicked hair and a smirk that didn't quite reach his eyes. His name was **Dean**.

Nia raised an eyebrow as she poured wine. Ella gave me a look — the kind that said, 'you feeling this too?'

Bridget was excited. "I've known Kate for ages — she's amazing. And Dean's a friend of hers. He's… curious."

I was warm and polite, but something about Dean was off. He spoke too easily. Too enthusiastically.

"Honestly," Dean grinned, "I don't care what's down there. Shaved, hairy, landing strip, full Amazon — it's all just a treat, isn't it?"

Ella went still.

I cleared my throat. "The Hedgerow isn't about kinks. It's about presence, pride, and how we're made to feel — especially women."

Dean waved a hand, brushing it off. "Course. Of course. I just mean, whatever gets people off, right? That's what this is?"

"No," said Nia, bluntly. "It's not."

Kate looked uncomfortable. She glanced at Dean, then down at her lap. "I didn't realise…"

I stood up slowly, setting down my drink. "Dean," I said evenly, "can I ask you something?"

Dean leaned back, grinning. "Go for it."

"What do you actually believe this is? What did Bridget tell you before you came?"

Dean shrugged. "She said it was a group about pubic hair. A kind of erotic throwback thing. I thought — sounds wild, why not?"

Bridget flushed. "That's not what I said. I said it was about the loss of something natural — and how people are reclaiming it. Not a 'wild thing'."

Dean gave a little chuckle. "Alright, alright. But come on — this is about sex, isn't it? About turning back time to when everyone was all wild and untrimmed and–"

"Stop," said Ella, rising from the sofa.

Dean blinked. "What?"

Ella stepped forward. "You're not listening. This isn't about nostalgia porn. It's not about getting your kicks from women who've chosen not to shave. It's about everything that was lost when society decided women should look prepubescent just to be considered sexy. This," she gestured around, "is about reclamation. About embodiment. And you don't belong here."

Dean snorted, standing now too. "Bit harsh, don't you think?"

"No," I said, my voice steely. "It's not. You came here with no respect. No care for what this is. You talked over Bridget. You reduced every woman here to a 'thing to get off on.' That's not Hedgerow. That's just the internet."

Bridget stepped between us, her voice firm but regretful. "Dean, I think you should go."

Dean looked at her, as if expecting her to take his side. But she didn't. She simply folded her arms.

He scoffed, muttered something about people being "too sensitive these days," and headed for the door.

Kate stood to follow him, but hesitated. "Could I stay?" she asked quietly. "I don't want to be part of what he is. I'm here for… this. For the right reasons."

I looked at Ella. Ella looked at Nia. Then back at Kate.

"Then yes," Ella said gently. "Stay."

The air in my flat felt different that evening. Dean was gone. The tension had shifted. A low playlist murmured in the background — all acoustic, soft rhythm and skin-close vocals. No one had spoken about what was next, but the energy was quietly unanimous.

Ella was the first to move. She stood and pulled her jumper over her head, slow and calm, revealing her body like it was the most natural act in the world. She didn't speak. She didn't need to.

Bridget followed, folding her top and setting it gently on the arm of the sofa.

Then Nia — bold as ever — tugged at the hem of her dress and slipped it free in one fluid motion, her bush proud and gleaming in the warm light. She didn't look for approval. She *was* approval.

Kate hesitated, but only for a second. Then she stood and said softly, "If I'm going to be part of this, I want to feel it fully." Her top joined the others. Her trousers followed.

Still seated, I felt the weight of the moment settle on me. I didn't reach for my clothes. Instead, I stood, unbuttoned my shirt, and said, "This is more than just pleasure. This is memory, honesty... body sovereignty."

We stood together, all five — each in different stages of undress. Not one body was the same. Not one story had followed the same path. But there they were, unhidden.

Ella stepped forward, brushing fingertips along Nia's hip, then reaching for Bridget's hand. Nia leaned into Kate, cheek brushing cheek. I stood, heart pounding, as arms and bodies drew together — not in chaos, but in choice.

The kiss that followed — slow, communal — was not about hunger. It was about returning. To truth. To joy. To something before the shame.

My arousal was proud and seen by all, yet I felt alive, where I belonged.

A tangle of limbs on cushions, light laughter, low sighs. We took turns. Touching, holding, teasing, asking. "May I?" "Yes." "There?" "Please."

The bush — the centrepiece, the catalyst — was no longer just hair. It was symbol. Softness. Wildness. Reclamation.

And by the time we curled into one another, the candlelight flickering low, the Hedgerow had grown another root.

Kate wasn't used to this — not just the nakedness, but the way no one stared. No one leered. No one compared or competed. It wasn't like the nights out she remembered in her twenties, where skin meant currency and interest came with a cost. This… was something else.

She sat beside Nia on the floor, backs against the base of the sofa, and let herself breathe.

Ella, ever the soft disruptor, leaned in gently, brushing a fingertip along Kate's forearm. "You alright?"

Kate nodded, voice low. "I feel like I've stepped through something."

Ella smiled. "You have."

I handed out glasses of wine, a touch of ceremony in the way I passed each one. "Tonight's not about categories," "But if you want to share how you identify, or how you don't, this is the room for it."

There was a silence — warm, not tense.

Kate sipped, then said, "I've only been with men. But I don't know if that's who I am, or just what I assumed I was allowed. I've wanted more. I just… never trusted the moment."

Ella moved closer and asked, "Would you trust it now, if it came from a woman you already feel safe with?"

Kate looked up, lips parted.

Nia leaned in, the flicker of mischief always on her face, and whispered, "She means me."

A ripple of laughter broke the tension, but Kate's eyes didn't waver. "Yes," she said. Quiet. Strong.

Nia didn't pounce — she closed the space gently, brushing a kiss along Kate's collarbone first. Kate tilted her head, accepting. Exploring.

Their mouths met. Not hungry — *curious*. Like they were finding out how two notes made a chord.

Meanwhile, Bridget had shifted beside me, stroking my chest in slow, absent patterns. We kissed, deeper this time, and Ella's hand wandered to join us. My breath hitched. This wasn't a performance. This was a pulse.

Bodies found each other. Not all at once, not in a frenzied tangle — but like vines slowly entwining in moonlight. Kate, now lying back with Nia between her legs, gasped softly as Nia's hair brushed her thighs. She laughed — a surprised, delighted laugh.

"She really does have a bush," she said, breathless.

Ella whispered back, "We all do. That's the point."

Kate came hard, trembling in a way that felt like release and relief at once. She pulled Nia up into a kiss, hands gripping her waist, her smile pure disbelief.

I watched from the cushions, Bridget's hand wrapped around my rock hard erection. "You alright?" she murmured,

I nodded. "Better than alright. This..yes ..yes..yes..then I came all over her hand. This is what it was always meant to be."

Nia and Kate curled together like ivy on brick — tangled, breathless, laughing now and then in those small, giddy bursts that come after release. Kate looked stunned in the softest way. Not from what had happened, but from what hadn't. No pressure. No spectacle. Just… being wanted, exactly as she was.

I laid on the rug beside Bridget, her head tucked into my shoulder, one leg draped over mine. Ella had pulled a blanket down from the sofa and wrapped herself in it, a hand resting lightly on my ankle, grounding us all.

Nobody said much now. There wasn't anything left to explain.

The wine sat unfinished on the table. The playlist had ended. Only the hush of breathing, the occasional sigh, the creak of the old radiator filled the room. The Hedgerow, once a wild idea, now had shape — and heat.

I watched the low light play across Ella's bare shoulder. She caught my glance, and with a small smile mouthed, 'You're not imagining this.'

And I wasn't.

Here, in the dim golden hush of my own flat, surrounded by those who had dared to show themselves fully, I felt something I hadn't in years — **honest arousal without shame**. And more than that, the beginning of a tribe. Not a cult of sex, nor a parade of parts, but a return to something rooted and ancient.

Bridget yawned. "Do we sleep here?"

Nia murmured, already half under. "Looks like it."

Ella tucked her blanket tighter. "This is what belonging feels like."

I didn't answer. I just reached for her hand beneath the wool, and held it.

Outside, the sky began to pale. Inside, five bodies lay tangled — quiet, safe, and full of the kind of promise no system had ever measured.

✦ ✦ ✦

Chapter 14
The First Reach

It began with a paragraph.

Not a manifesto. Not a shout. Just a paragraph, carefully shaped by me and Ella one damp Thursday afternoon. The rain tapped steadily on the glass as if checking we were sure.

We sat opposite each other in the quiet of my kitchen, laptops open, both hesitant to type the first word.

Ella sipped her coffee and stared into the steam. "What if we didn't call it anything?"

I looked up. "No name?"

"No movement. No title. Just a feeling."

I nodded. That felt truer somehow. Less like a campaign, more like a crack in the noise — something that only the right people would hear.

Together, we shaped the words slowly. We didn't mention body hair. We didn't mention sex. Just the feeling of absence. The sense of having been flattened, tidied, streamlined until something rich and unnamable had quietly disappeared.

"If you've ever felt unseen because you chose not to follow a trend…
If you've ever been told you'd be beautiful if only you changed something…
If you've felt the creeping sense that desire no longer belongs to your

kind of body —
We're listening.

Not everyone will understand this.
But if you do — you'll know exactly why it's here."

We posted it anonymously in an obscure, reflective Reddit thread titled 'Feminine Without Permission'. A quiet corner. Mostly forgotten. That felt right.

Then we waited.

Three days later, a message came in.

It arrived just after midnight. I read it alone, backlit by the glow of my screen.

"I read your message and I can't stop shaking.
I haven't let myself think about this for years.
I used to keep my hair. I loved how it felt — how it made me feel.
But I gave up. Every man I was with called it 'retro' or said it
'wasn't for them.' I stopped asking. I stopped even feeling.
But what you wrote — I don't know how to explain it.
I just knew it was for me.
If you are real… please write back.
– Rose"

I stared at the screen for a long time. The tone was raw, careful. She hadn't asked for pictures. She hadn't said anything performative. Just truth.

I forwarded it to Ella and the others immediately.

The next evening, we gathered.

Lara was the first to speak. "She's one of us. I can tell. That message— I read it three times. She's felt what I've felt."

Tom folded his arms, not in defiance, but in thought. "We said we'd be careful. What if this goes wrong?"

Bridget leaned forward. "We've been careful. Maybe too careful. If we wait for everyone to be vouched for, we'll just recreate the same circle again and again."

Ella looked to me. "She feels real. And honest. And she's been alone with this. For years, probably."

I nodded slowly. "I say we invite her. Not to a full gathering — not yet. Just to meet. Maybe here. Just her, and whoever feels comfortable."

Everyone agreed. The invitation was sent that night, soft in tone but firm in boundaries:
'A conversation first. Nothing more. No expectations. Just presence.'

The bell rang just after six.

I opened the door and there she was — Rose.She stood with both hands wrapped around the strap of her faded satchel, hair damp from the drizzle, eyes searching my face with a quiet urgency. She looked to be in her early forties, with a softness that had nothing to do with appearance and everything to do with energy — that quietly uncertain way some women enter a room after years of being told they take up too much space.

I smiled gently. "You found us."

She nodded, exhaled, and stepped inside.

The room was warm, dimly lit by golden lamps and the soft glow of candles. No incense. No ambient music. Just the crackle of the fire and the murmured clink of tea cups being set down.

Everyone had arrived early.

Ella, barefoot as always, greeted Rose first. "Welcome. You're safe here. We're not here to test you or ask you to perform. Just sit. Be."

Bridget added, "This is for *you* as much as it is for us. You're the first to come from outside. That matters."

Tom gave a polite nod, staying back slightly, sensing the delicacy of the moment. Lara smiled, wide-eyed and kind, while Kate quietly slid a cushion beside her own and gestured gently.

Then Nia stood — vivid, tall, unashamed in her presence — and walked straight to Rose.

"I'm Nia," she said. "And I want you to know… it's okay if you're scared. Most of us were, at the start. But something told you to come. That's all we need to know."

Rose's eyes filled instantly. Not in embarrassment — in release.

She dropped her satchel slowly, then whispered, "I didn't think people like this… existed. Not really."

"You do now," Nia said, and gently took her hand.

We sat in a loose circle, warm mugs in hand. No one rushed to speak. It was Rose who broke the silence first.

"When I was younger," she said, voice steadying, "I had this boyfriend. He used to call me his forest. Said I was wild and ancient and beautiful. I never forgot that." She gave a small, private smile. "But then things changed. Not just with him — with everything. The comments got sharper. The expectations tighter. Suddenly my body wasn't just mine anymore. It was something to be… modified."

I leaned forward, my tone low. "That forest never left you. It just waited for the right season."

That was when Rose cried. Openly, without apology. And this time, no one moved to hush it. Nia reached for her hand again. Kate passed a tissue. Lara rubbed her back gently.

And in that moment, something shifted.

This wasn't just a group of like-minded friends anymore.

This was a **movement**.

It had grown its first root outside the circle — and it had been met not with fear, but with tears, truth, and the slow reawakening of pride.

The tears passed like a wave — deep but brief. Rose dabbed her eyes, laughed softly, and looked around.

"This is going to sound ridiculous," she said, "but I don't actually know what I've walked into."

A few of us smiled. Not mockingly — with recognition. Ella leaned forward.

"It's not ridiculous. That's part of what makes this work — we never advertise it clearly. We just... let the energy draw the right people."

Rose nodded slowly. "Right. And I knew, reading that message, that something in me ached for it. I just—" She glanced toward me, then back to Ella. "I didn't know if it was emotional, political, or… something else."

Bridget took a breath and said gently, "It's all of those. And yes — there's a sexual layer. Not in the way some might expect, but it's there. It's real."

"We're not a sex club," Lara added quickly. "It's not about performing or hooking up. It's about reclaiming a kind of unfiltered presence — and for many of us, that includes how we relate to our erotic selves."

Tom spoke next, voice careful. "Everything happens with choice. With consent. No pressure. Some gatherings are just talks, some are storytelling… and sometimes they go deeper. But only when it's mutual, natural, and true."

Rose exhaled. "I think… I knew that. I felt it in the words. There was something…" She hesitated. "It wasn't titillating. It was alive. Like a part of me wanted to reach through the screen and whisper, 'Take me with you.'"

Nia gave a low chuckle. "That's exactly what we heard."

I watched Rose's face carefully. "You're not here to be anything. You don't have to prove or reveal or even stay, if it doesn't feel right. This space bends to the energy of whoever's in it."

"I'd like to stay," Rose said. "Just to sit. To listen."

Ella raised her cup in silent welcome. We all followed, one by one.

And with that, the circle held — now wider, warmer, and quietly lit by the awareness that their erotic current, once private, had reached someone entirely new… and been met not with suspicion, but recognition.

The fire crackled softly as the room settled into silence again.
Rose looked down at her untouched tea, then back up at the circle of faces waiting — not expectant, but open.

She swallowed. "There's something I want to tell you. I don't know if it's the sort of thing you say aloud in a room full of strangers, but…"

Ella smiled. "Try us."

Rose took a breath, tucked her knees underneath her, and began.

"I was nineteen when I met a woman named Marianne. She was ten years older than me — worked in the university archive, of all places. We met because I kept losing my ID card. She told me I needed to slow down. Said everything about me moved too fast."

She paused, her voice warming. "She had thick black hair, and she smelled like cedarwood and something else I could never place. Anyway — I'd never been with a woman before. I didn't even know I wanted to be. But she made me feel seen. Not ogled. Not praised. Seen."

There were a few slow nods. Kate shifted slightly closer.

Rose's voice dropped to a quieter register. "The first time I undressed in front of her, I was embarrassed. I hadn't shaved anything. I'd never even tried. She looked at me, just looked, and then said, 'There you are.' Not 'there it is.' Not a compliment. Not a joke. Just… there you are."

She paused, letting that line hang in the air.

"I've never forgotten it. Because it was the first time my body felt like a presence, not a compromise. And after her — after Marianne — I thought I'd carry that feeling forever."

She looked up, more composed now. "But it didn't last. I fell into the world. Dating apps. Comments. Quiet little phrases that chipped away at it. 'You're brave, keeping it natural.' 'It's very… European of you.' That kind of thing. At first, I joked it off. Then I started booking waxes. One by one, I let those parts of me vanish."

Rose let out a breath, almost a laugh. "I even convinced myself I liked it. Told myself it was more 'tidy,' more 'clean.' I bought into the language. I cut myself off from my own memory."

Nia was watching intently. "Until you didn't."

Rose looked at her. "Until I didn't. Until I read that post and something in me cracked open. I remembered Marianne. I remembered that moment. I remembered *me*. And I realised… I didn't want to fit in anymore. I wanted to return."

There was a hush. A reverent pause.

"I don't know where this is going," Rose finished. "I don't know if I'm brave enough to be as open as you lot. But I know I belong here. And I know I'm ready to stop pretending that the wildest part of me was some kind of mistake."

Ella reached for her hand.

"You're already one of us."

And for the first time since she arrived, Rose smiled with certainty. Not gratitude. Not awe. Just the quiet, unmistakable glow of someone reclaiming herself — fully, fiercely, and without apology.

There was a long silence after Rose's story, the kind that doesn't ask to be filled — it just settles over the room like velvet.

But then, something shifted in her posture. She placed her mug down on the floor and looked around the circle, cheeks flushing but eyes steady.

"I need to show you," she said. "Not to be provocative. Not even to be erotic. I just… if I'm going to be part of this, I want to show you that it's real again. That I didn't just remember. I returned."

No one spoke. We didn't need to. The group held space — open, warm, respectful.

Rose slowly rose to her feet.

She unbuttoned her jeans without fanfare, hooked her thumbs beneath the waistband, and eased them down, along with her simple cotton underwear. Then she stood tall, letting her blouse fall loosely to her hips, everything else bare.

And there it was.

A full, rich bush — dark and proud, soft at the edges and wild at the centre. It hadn't been sculpted or shaped. It was nature's own, grown back with quiet resolve and the kind of care that no one ever talks about. Not for display. Not for approval. Just because it was meant to be there.

I felt the weight of the moment. It wasn't about lust — it was about recognition. This wasn't a show. This was **ritual**.

Bridget was the first to move — not toward her, but in solidarity. She rose to her feet and, without a word, untied her dress and let it fall. Her bush was red-gold and untamed, curling up her thighs like vines.

Then Nia stood, strong and magnificent, peeling down her loose trousers with a grin. "Welcome to the garden," she said.

Lara followed, then Ella, then Kate — each one joining not to perform, but to stand with her.

Tom didn't move. He didn't need to. He watched with adulation , the only man in the room besides me, both of us choosing stillness over assertion.

Finally, Rose looked down at herself… then up again. "This," she said quietly, "was gone for fifteen years. And now it's back. And I'm never shaving it again."

A low hum of approval ran through the room. Not applause. Something deeper.

Ella crossed to her, kissed her cheek, and whispered, "You've planted yourself. Now let's see how you bloom."

Rose looked around at the standing women, then turned her gaze to me and Tom — still seated, still watching.

Her voice was calm, but clear. "Why are you two still down there?"

Neither of us flinched. I met her gaze with a slight smile, not defensive, but thoughtful.

Tom spoke first, his voice low. "Because this wasn't about us. This was your moment. Yours to reclaim."

I added, "We've already taken up enough space in other parts of the world. This — this garden — is one we wanted to honour, not enter uninvited."

Rose tilted her head. "You think standing beside us would be an intrusion?"

There was a pause. Tom looked to me, then back to her. "Only if it's not welcome."

Rose held their gaze, then smiled — not softly, but with mischief. "Well, I'm welcoming it. I've shown you mine. Don't make me think you're only here to admire from a distance."

Ella laughed, low and delighted. "She's definitely one of us."

I stood first, slow and deliberate. I didn't rush. I didn't hesitate. I simply rose, stepped forward, and undid my belt.

There was no bravado, no tension. Just truth.

I let my trousers fall to the floor, standing in full view, my body relaxed and upright, framed by the firelight.

And just like that, I was part of the moment — not as a voyeur, but as a participant.

Tom stepped into the light, his eyes lowered at first, then lifting slightly as he exhaled and let his trousers fall.

There was a brief, unmistakable pause in the room — not out of shock, but awareness. Tom stood there, quietly composed, and yes — notably well-endowed. Not in a showy way, not exaggerated. Just… confidently present, unashamed, like the rest of him.

It was Nia who broke the silence — with a grin tugging at the corner of her mouth.

"Well," she said, tilting her head and pretending to fan herself with one hand, "we did say the Hedgerow was about growth."

We all burst into soft, warm laughter — not mean-spirited, not mocking. Just the kind of laughter that lets the body breathe again.

Tom chuckled and rubbed the back of his neck. "Not quite what I expected to be known for."

Nia winked. "Oh don't worry, love — it's not the size that matters. But if it happens to be a lovely surprise, I say we acknowledge it."

Rose was laughing too now, relaxed and feeling aroused at his manhood. Not too sure how to respond. 'Should I move forward to touch it'? 'Should I get on my knees and say put it in my mouth'? Or should I just respect the moment? 'Rose decided on the latter.

I added, with a smile, "Another natural wonder joins the garden." As I gingerly looked down at my own penis. Just kind of languorous.

And with that, the circle closed — not in exclusivity, but in completion. Bodies present.

Desires acknowledged. Dignity intact.

✦ ✦ ✦

Chapter 15
Beyond the Garden Wall

It had grown faster than any of us expected.

What began as seven bodies in a firelit room — skin bare, stories raw, laughter honest — was now a swelling tide of names, messages, sign-ups, and strangers claiming allegiance to *The Hedgerow*.

Within weeks of Rose's arrival, the group had quietly welcomed others. Some came through new posts, others through whispered recommendations, or hushed late-night DMs that simply said:
"I think I'm one of you."

I stopped counting at seventy-three. Ella said it hit a hundred by mid-month.

At first, the expansion felt thrilling. Each new member brought another story — another reclaiming. A teacher who'd shaved daily for thirty years. A mother who cried when her daughter asked if body hair was "allowed." A man who had never dared speak aloud what he longed for most.

But then, the shift.

A new thread appeared online:
"The Hedgerow isn't just personal — it's political."

Another called it a **movement against enforced grooming culture**, then another pushed harder:
"This is the new erotic resistance."

"End patriarchal waxing."
"Shave shame is oppression."

Flyers were made.
Podcasts began.
And suddenly, people none of them had ever met were speaking on their behalf.

Ella was the first to say it out loud. "This isn't what we built. This is… something else."

I agreed. "We were a sanctuary. Not a rebellion."

Bridget added, "They're taking the most intimate thing we ever made — and using it like a banner."

Even Nia, ever bold, was wary now. "They're not wrong about the politics. But we didn't give them permission to use our bodies like proof."

The Hedgerow had become a headline.
But in doing so, it had started to lose its heart.

Rose changed slowly.

At first, it was in her language — just small shifts.
Where once she spoke of sensation, she now spoke of sacrifice.
Where once she laughed easily, she now talked of symbols and cause.

She started posting more frequently than any of us. Quotes that none of us had said. Phrases that made my stomach twist.

"We are the wild truth they tried to scrape away."
"Every wax strip is a wound."
"Men who ask for smoothness are enemies of the flesh."

It wasn't that the words were entirely false — it was that they weren't ours

And then came the stories.

Rose began telling dramatic, sometimes disturbing tales during gatherings — of lovers who'd mocked her, of men who'd rejected her violently for her bush, of friendships ruined by razor blades. But the tone was off. Too polished. Too well-timed. Too perfect.

Bridget was the first to question it privately.
"She said the man slapped her and left because she had pubic hair," Bridget whispered to Ella. "But last week she said he cried and told her she reminded him of his mother. That's not a detail you forget."

Ella nodded, lips pressed into a thin line. "She's not just remembering anymore. She's building something."

I brought it up the next evening. The founders met in his living room, the room where it all began — the cushions still on the floor, though now slightly threadbare from too many newcomers.

"She's being pushed," I said. "I've seen this before. Someone gets swept up in a cause and someone behind the scenes starts feeding them language. Images. Talking points."

Nia frowned. "By who?"

"That's the thing. I don't think it's public. I think it's private. Organised. Someone's feeding her this."

Tom leaned forward. "You think she's in contact with a group?"

"I think there's something like a centre," I said, quietly. "A place. Not physical, necessarily. But… strategic. A pressure point."

Ella folded her arms. "If it's true, they've found a perfect mouthpiece. She's emotional, articulate — and wounded. That makes her powerful."

"And vulnerable," Lara added.

There was silence again.

Then Bridget said it aloud:
"She's becoming dangerous. Not intentionally — but still."

She continued. "I don't want to accuse her. I just want to know if *we* are still safe in our own space."

Tom nodded. "Same. We don't burn the garden to get rid of one weed."

I looked toward Ella, who hadn't said much since the meeting began. She was staring into the fire, legs tucked beneath her, quiet.

Then she spoke.

"We invite her to a special session. One designed for her. Private. Small. No pressure, no removal of clothing. Just storytelling. Something she can't resist."

Bridget caught on quickly. "We let her lead the circle."

"And we plant a detail," Ella added. "A moment that never happened. Something tender. True-sounding. But fictional."

I sat forward. "And then we wait. If that detail shows up in one of her public posts, interviews, or stories outside the circle… we'll know she's been leaking. Or worse — performing."

Lara glanced around the room. "That's the trap? Just a lie?"

Ella smiled softly. "Not a lie. A thread. And we'll see who pulls it."

Tom offered, "What if it's about me? Something believable. Like… I once whispered to her that her bush reminded me of my first love. That I wept. That I said she'd healed something in me."

Nia gave a low chuckle. "That's almost too poetic."

I nodded. "But it's good. It's human. Tender. And it would only have happened *in private*."

Bridget added, "And we all agree — it never happened. If we see it anywhere else, we know."

Ella looked around the group. "No confrontation. No drama. We just watch. And if she crosses the line… then we talk. As founders. As a circle."

We all nodded.

The trap wasn't cruel. It wasn't loud.
It was, in its way, the purest kind of truth — a test of respect.

And in that moment, the founders of the Hedgerow became guardians of something we hadn't expected to need defending.

Not just the bush.
But the integrity that gave it power.

I left the city at dawn.

No dramatic departure, no announcement. Just a holdall, a train ticket, and a quiet ache for something simpler. I found a converted barn-inn nestled at the edge of a valley, all wildflowers, bees, and creaky floorboards. The kind of place that smelled like wood smoke and old linen.

I didn't bring a laptop. I didn't answer messages. I walked. I breathed. I listened to silence again.

And on the second night, I met **Maya**.

She was sitting alone in the small guest lounge, reading by firelight in bare feet, curls tied up with a scarf. Our conversation began over a shared bottle of red, then drifted into books, solitude, the need to switch off. She, too, had come for quiet.

Later — back in her room, clothes loose and wine warm in their veins — the conversation softened into touch.

And when her dress slid away, when her knickers followed, I saw it: a soft, shapely bush — grown fully, naturally, without hesitation.

My breath caught slightly. I didn't hide it.

"I'm sorry," I said, smiling. "I just… it's beautiful. You've kept it."

Maya raised an eyebrow, amused. "You sound surprised."

"Most are shaved," I replied gently. "Or sculpted. You… you haven't bowed to that."

She chuckled. "Oh, I used to. God, I used to. But I stopped about a year ago."

I kissed her thigh. "May I ask what changed?"

Maya sighed, her hand lazily stroking my hair. "A woman I know — not a friend, just someone who kept showing up in certain circles — she started making noise about this underground group called *The Hedgerow*."

I froze.

"She said it was full of sexual deviants," Maya continued casually. "Some erotic cult of people with 'body hair fetishes' trying to spread their influence through online grooming. Her words, not mine."

I lifted my head. "What was her name?"

She thought for a moment. "Rose, I think. Rose Withers, maybe? Pale, serious. Always had that I've-seen-the-truth-and-you-haven't energy."

I sat up slowly.

Maya noticed. "Why? Is that a name I shouldn't have said?"

I shook my head. "No. It's just… I know her. Or I thought I did."

Maya studied me for a moment, then smiled softly.

"Well, if you're part of whatever that Hedgerow thing really is… I hope you keep it alive. Because I never felt more myself than when I stopped shaving and let men deal with it."

I gave a small laugh. "We're trying. Or at least… we were."

I lay back down beside her, heart thrumming — not from sex, not from wine, but from realisation.

Rose hadn't just lost her way.

She was actively working against us.

And now, I had proof.

✦ ✦ ✦

Chapter 16
The Bush Never Lies

I returned late Sunday evening, mud still on my boots and a strange calm clinging to me like mist.

I didn't go home. I went straight to Ella's.

By the time I arrived, the others were already there — Bridget, Tom, Nia, Lara, and Kate — seated in the candlelit living room they now referred to, half-jokingly, as 'the root chamber.' Rose hadn't been invited.

No one needed to ask why.

The detail — the trap they had carefully planted — had appeared.

That morning, Bridget had sent a screenshot to the group chat. A long, polished paragraph in a body-positivity forum written by someone named *R.W.*. In it, she described a Hedgerow member named Tom who had once wept, naked, as he confessed that her pubic hair reminded him of his first love — and healed a lifetime of shame.

It was word for word.

Tom had never said it.
The moment had never happened.
And only **Rose** had been told the lie.

Now I stood before them, coat still on, heart steady. "It's her," I said simply. "There's no doubt."

Ella nodded. "We saw the leak."

"There's more," I added. "I met someone while I was away — a woman named Maya. Total stranger. She had a bush, proudly. When I commented on it, she mentioned a woman named Rose who's been showing up online… not just mocking the Hedgerow, but calling us a kind of grooming cult."

Lara sat back, stunned. "So she's not just twisting stories — she's actively trying to dismantle us."

"Then Nia, ever still, ever watchful, reached for her tea, took a slow sip, and said:

"The bush never lies."

There was a beat.

Then laughter. Small at first — a ripple of release.

Bridget wiped her eyes. "Bloody hell, Nia."

"No, I'm serious," Nia said, grinning. "Bodies tell the truth. Always. Hers said she belonged. But her mouth… that's another matter."

I finally sat. "She's building something outside of us. Something louder. Something corrupt. And she's dragging the Hedgerow name through it."

Ella looked around the circle. "So what do we do now?"

Kate, who hadn't spoken yet, whispered, "We reclaim the root."

We all looked at her.

"We take it back," she said, stronger now. "Not by fighting Rose. Not with public posts or rebuttals. We return to what made it sacred — real bodies, real presence, real truth. The Hedgerow isn't a cause. It's a place. A way. A witnessing."

I nodded. "And we begin with the next gathering. Carefully. Quietly. But this time, we lead."

✦ ✦ ✦

Chapter 17
The Reckoning in the Hedgerow

We called it *The Gathering of the row* — an evening of reconnection, storytelling, and shared presence.

Forty members. Some new. Some old. Most had never met beyond fleeting nods or private messages. It was the largest event the Hedgerow had ever held.

It took place in a hired retreat hall — wood floors, low lighting, tall windows open to a dark meadow. There were candles, cushions, bowls of fresh fruit. Quiet music played on a loop — strings and silence.

Rose arrived wearing soft grey linen, her hair tied back in a braid. She moved through the space like someone familiar with admiration. She greeted others confidently, laughing lightly, even kissing cheeks.

I noticed that she looked completely at ease. Too at ease. As if she'd already written the post about the night in her head — long before it had begun.

Ella, Bridget, Tom, and the others mingled too, keeping their distance at first. But they were watching. The trap was not physical. It was atmospheric.

And at the centre of it — the twist.

At 8:30, Ella stood up, barefoot, glass in hand.

"Welcome, Hedgerow kin," she said. "Tonight isn't just a gathering. It's a re-rooting. A return to the soil we started from. And to honour that, we've invited seven voices to speak."

She smiled. "Seven stories. Seven truths. All of them… completely made up."

A ripple passed through the crowd. Some smiled, intrigued. Others looked confused.

Rose's brow furrowed, just slightly.

Ella continued. "These stories were crafted in private — fiction told as if real. They were offered to individuals in deep trust, with one instruction: to remain held within the Hedgerow."

She let that linger.

I stepped forward. "But one of them didn't stay. One of them left our roots. It appeared outside the garden. Word for word. Under someone else's name."

Now Rose blinked. She tried to mask it — but her posture shifted. Her fingers curled around her wine glass a little too tightly.

Bridget added, "This isn't punishment. It's witnessing. We built this on trust. And someone, knowingly or not, broke that trust."

Tom stood. "So tonight, we're reading the stories aloud. All of them. Including the one that left the garden."

Murmurs moved through the room.

Rose said nothing. But her expression had changed. No longer smug. No longer glowing. Just… still.

Ella finished, "There will be no naming. No accusation. We will simply speak. And in the silence that follows, everyone will know."

Ella lit a tall beeswax candle in the centre of the room. The room dimmed. The music faded.

I stepped forward with the first card in hand.

Story One: "The Cinnamon Bath"

I spoke slowly, my voice low and rich.

"She invited me to her flat after work. Said she'd made a bath just for me — cinnamon oil and clary sage. The smell hit me before I reached the bedroom. Steam drifted down the hall like it had a body of its own.

She undressed me slowly — not just the clothes but the day. My anger. My tension. My ego.

And then, when I stepped into the water, she knelt beside the tub... and kissed my knee.

Just that. Nothing more.

But in that moment, I broke. Not from lust. From the weightlessness of it. She didn't try to fix me. She just held me... right there, with the scent of bark and salt on my skin, and her mouth on my bones."

The room was still. The air, heavy.

I placed the card back on the table and sat down.

Story Two: "The Gorse Field"
Read by Bridget.

"We lay in a field of gorse, half-dressed, half-sunk into the earth. The sun had turned my shoulders pink, and the grass beneath us was still warm from the afternoon.

She told me not to speak. Just to watch her.

And I did. I watched as she took off her trousers and let her bush catch the wind like wild grass — thick, golden, alive. She stood above me like a pagan idol, fingers trailing her own thighs, not for my benefit but her own.

Then she laughed — deep, guttural — and climbed onto me.

We didn't fuck. We woke something. Her hands dug into the soil. Mine into her hips. We smelled like pollen and sweat and sunburn, and when she came, she bit my shoulder like she was planting her name there."

A few people in the room shifted, breath shallow.

No one spoke.

Story Three: "Tom's Tear"
Read by Ella, slowly, deliberately.

"He cried when I touched him. Not sobbing. Just tears — wet and unexpected.

He said my bush reminded him of his first love — a girl with dark hair and a defiant laugh, someone who let her body grow like a secret she didn't need to hide.

He said he hadn't touched anyone like me in years. That he didn't even realise how much he'd missed this — this softness, this truth.

And when he came, he held me like he was afraid I'd vanish."

Ella looked up after finishing.

No one clapped. No one moved.

Tom simply said, "That moment never happened. Not to me. Not with anyone here. And yet, two days ago, it appeared on a public forum. Almost word for word."

The air tightened.

I stood again. "We won't say who shared it. But everyone now knows… someone did. And that person changed the Hedgerow — from inside."

As the third story ended — Tom's Tear — the silence in the room grew dense. Nobody moved, but everyone felt the shift.

And that's when Rose stood.

Not abruptly. Not angrily. Just… deliberately. She placed her wine glass on a nearby table. Picked up her wrap. Adjusted her braid.

She moved with elegance — the kind that wants to appear calm while nerves crack just beneath the surface.

She didn't look at anyone.

But everyone saw her.

She walked to the edge of the circle, stepped lightly around cushions and outstretched feet, and reached the door.

She paused, just for a second, one hand on the handle.
Ella's eyes met mine.
Bridget didn't blink.
Nia raised a single eyebrow.

Then Rose slipped out into the night.

The door clicked shut behind her.

No one followed.

Tom exhaled. "She heard it."

Ella nodded. "And she knows we heard it too."

Lara whispered, "Do we call her back?"

"No, "I said, quietly. "That was the calling."

Nia finished her herbal tea, still watching the door. "The bush never lies. But people do. And she just showed us who she was."

The candle flame flickered in the stillness.

Ella stood again. "We'll finish the readings. Not for her. For us. Because this is what we protect. Not a name. Not a brand. But the body of truth we grow together."

One by one, the members shifted upright again.

No outrage. No argument.

Just the sound of breath, bare skin brushing cushions, and the slow turning of story cards — as the Hedgerow quietly, powerfully, returned to itself.

✦ ✦ ✦

Interlude – The Undoing

Rose slammed the door behind her.

The hallway echoed with her footsteps — sharp, decisive, unnatural. She didn't drop her bag, didn't take off her shoes. She went straight to the bathroom.

Bright lights. White tiles. Cold porcelain. No candles. No warmth. Just the harsh reflection of herself in the mirror.

She didn't cry.

Not once.

She opened the drawer. Pulled out the razor. The foam.

Her braid fell over one shoulder as she peeled off her trousers. Her underwear. She looked down at what had once been her pride — the full, dark bush she had praised in public, flaunted in interviews, described in lyrical detail to people who wanted to believe she meant it.

Now, it felt like a costume.

She lathered it in silence.

Each stroke of the razor came fast, almost careless. The foam turned pink in places. She didn't flinch.

By the time she was finished, the floor was wet. Her thighs were trembling. Her skin blotched with tiny cuts and stinging patches.

She stared at herself in the mirror.

Bald. Exposed. Blank.

Then she whispered — to no one —

"There. Now no one can say I was ever one of them."

She wrapped a towel around her waist and left the room without switching off the light.

The following morning, I looked around the room — at the cushions, the candle, the mugs cooling beside bare thighs and crossed legs.

And then, almost to myself, I said:

"This is how it started. Right here. Nia, Ella, and me. At this kitchen table."

Ella glanced at me, a slow smile forming. "The first three."

Nia chuckled softly. "We didn't even know what we were growing. Just that it felt like soil."

Wow! But what a night we had, hey?

Bridget leaned back in her chair, running her fingers along the candleholder. "And now look."

I nodded. "We've lost people. Gained others. Been misunderstood. But this—" I gestured around the room, at the ease, the skin, the breath. "This is *The Hedgerow*. Not what we post. Not what they say. This."

The room was quiet again.

Not heavy. Just whole.

And the candle flickered once — steady, soft, and unafraid.

Chapter 18
The First Flame

It was Nia who said it first.

"We should tell it. The beginning."

We were still in Ella's kitchen. The others had drifted off — to walk the garden path, to stretch in the sunlight. But the three of us remained: Me, Ella, and Nia. The first flame.

No one moved to get dressed.

I was still naked, leaning back in a chair, feet flat on the floor. Ella wore nothing but the blanket she'd barely bothered to wrap. Nia, as ever, sat proudly bare, her legs folded like a sculpture — warm, unashamed, rooted.

There was no tension in our nudity. No charge. Just truth.

Ella reached across the table and touched my wrist. "You remember what you said? That night?"

I nodded. "I said I was tired of performance. Of everything being an angle. Even sex felt like theatre. And I didn't want theatre anymore."

Nia smiled. "You said you wanted to look at someone without wondering what they'd post about it later."

I exhaled. "And you said—"

"I said, 'Then let's stop performing.'"

We all laughed softly.

Ella stood slowly and walked to the window. "I was the first to undress."

"You were," I said, watching her.

"And I didn't do it seductively. I just took off my jumper. Then my jeans. Then I stood there, barefoot on these bloody tiles, and said: 'Is this what you meant?'"

"And it was," Nia said. "Exactly."

I remembered the moment clearly — the silence that followed, not awkward but electric. The way Ella stood with her arms at her sides, not covering, not posing. Just present.

Then Nia had risen and undressed too. Her body was taller, darker, fuller. When she dropped her clothes, she didn't say a word. She just sat down at the table again — stark, dignified, like a queen without a throne. I had hesitated. Of course I had. A man undressing before two women — it came with every possible caution, every layer of history.

But they had watched me as equals. Not with invitation. Not with fear. Just… waiting.

And so I had stood. Folded my shirt. Unfastened my trousers. Let everything go — clothes, hesitation, the armor I didn't even know I was still wearing.

Then we had sat. Three naked people at a kitchen table. No sex. No pressure. Just skin, breath, eyes, and the beginning of something they hadn't yet named.

We sat in the quiet that followed — the kind of silence that only came after a deep truth was spoken.

I leaned back in my chair, eyes half-lidded, staring at the floorboards as if they held the memory. My breath had deepened. Slower now. But heavier.

I felt it before I acknowledged it — the heat rising, the pulse shifting. Arousal. Uninvited, unforced… and absolutely real.

Nia noticed first. She didn't speak — just watched me, a subtle curl of a smile at the corner of her mouth. Her eyes dipped, once, then rose again.

Ella followed her gaze. And then looked at me — fully, without flinching.

I noticed.

I flushed slightly. "Sorry— I…"

Ella cut me off gently. "Don't."

Nia leaned in on her elbows. "That's not something we apologise for in the Hedgerow. Especially not here."

I exhaled through my nose, a small embarrassed laugh escaping. "I don't even know what triggered it."

"Yes, you do," Nia said.

Ella's voice was softer now. "We were naked. Together. Around this table. And it wasn't a performance. It was… real. The first time you'd ever been seen like that — without needing to be wanted, or impressive, or strong."

I swallowed. "It made me feel… open. And wanted. Not for anything I did. Just… as I was."

"And it still does," Nia said, eyes fixed on me.

My arousal was no longer something subtle now. It stood there, between them, present. Not vulgar. Not ashamed. Just… truth.

Ella reached across the table again, this time brushing her fingers along my forearm — not suggestively, not with expectation. Just contact. Real.

"You're allowed to feel," she said. "Even if it shows."

My eyes closed for a moment. My breath shook.

Then Nia stood, walked slowly around the table, and stood behind me. She placed her hands on my shoulders. Her thumbs pressed gently at the base of my neck — grounding me.

"You were the seed," she said. "That night, you brought it to life. You were open, and so we opened too. That's what this was always about."

Ella stood as well, coming around to my side, her hand now resting just above my heart.

Three bodies. Naked. Breathing.

Not rushing.

Just remembering… and feeling.

My breath caught as Nia's hands moved from my shoulders to my collarbone, fingers spreading slowly, warmly, like someone tracing a shape she already knew.

Ella knelt beside me, her palm still resting just over my heart — steady, present. She looked up at me, eyes soft, lips parted slightly. "You're allowed to be touched, too."

I exhaled — a slow, trembling sound that released something deeper than tension.

I nodded.

That was all it took.

Nia leaned forward, her full breasts brushing my back, her lips now close to my ear. "Let us see you," she whispered.

Ella's hand drifted down my chest, slow and sure, fingertips grazing the faint trail of hair that led to the part of me already awake. She didn't rush. She simply explored — not to arouse further, but to witness.

I stood.

I didn't mean to. My body just rose, like it needed to move. My arousal stood proud and exposed now, no longer something to hide — but something to honour.

Nia came to face me, her hand tracing down my arm, then taking my hand in hers.

Ella moved behind me now, her hands exploring my back, hips, thighs — her mouth brushing the top of my spine, then lower.

Nia kissed my sternum. Not hungrily — admiringly. Then lower. A kiss to my navel. Then to my hip. Then to the space beside my cock, not yet touching it.

I trembled.

"You're still listening," she whispered.

"To what?" I breathed.

"To your body. That's all we ever asked of anyone."

And then — finally — her mouth wrapped around the full erect cock, slow, warm, and patient.

I gasped — not just from sensation, but from the receiving. The way it was given. Not taken. Not earned. Just offered.

Ella came to my side, her lips at my neck now, her hand cradling my thigh as Nia moved rhythmically below. No words. Just presence. Breath. Warm skin. Hair brushing my inner leg.

My hands moved instinctively — one on Ella's shoulder, the other in Nia's hair. Not to guide. Just to anchor.

And as I began to tremble, thighs tightening, breath catching — Ella whispered:

"Let go. You're safe."

And I did.

I came in Nia's mouth with a low, guttural sound — part moan, part surrender — held between them, body shaking, heart wide open. Cum dripping from the corner of Nia's mouth.

When it was done, Nia rose slowly, kissed my chest again. Ella stroked my cheek.

No laughter. No awkwardness. Just **skin**, and **truth**, and a man who had finally allowed himself to be received in full.

I sat back on the cushion, breath still slowing, skin tingling. My body felt light, open — emptied in the best way.

Nia remained kneeling beside me. Ella sat across from her, their eyes meeting in a way that was older than speech.

No signal was given. No permission asked.

Ella leaned forward and kissed Nia — soft at first, then with a growing hunger that pulsed from deep within.

Their hands found each other's faces. Then necks. Then hips.

I watched, still naked, still grounded, still dripping. But now… entranced.

Nia reached for Ella's breast, cupping it gently, thumb brushing the nipple until it hardened beneath her touch. Ella gasped, tilted her head back slightly, and Nia's mouth followed — kissing, sucking, grazing with teeth.

Ella moaned — not for me, not for show — but for Nia. For the touch she had wanted for longer than she'd ever said aloud.

Then Ella pushed Nia gently onto her back and moved between her legs, parting them slowly, longingly, revealing a bush just as full and radiant as her own. Ella bent low and began to kiss her — not just between her thighs, but along her inner leg, her hipbone, the edge of her mound.

My cock stirred again, heavy now with the slow return of desire. I didn't touch myself. I didn't need to. Watching was enough. It was everything.

I watched Ella bury her mouth in Nia's centre, tongue slow and knowing. Nia arched, hands tangled in hair, whispering her name again and again.

The room was thick with breath and scent — raw, rich, and unmistakably human.

And that's when the front door opened.

A hush of footsteps. Laughter.

Then Bridget's voice. "Ella? We brought—"

They stopped.

Bridget. Lara. Tom.

Standing in the doorway, caught between surprise and recognition.

What they saw:
Ella, between Nia's legs, hair falling down her back.
Me, seated naked, watching — hard again, unabashed.
Candles flickering. Bodies glistening.
The Hedgerow alive.

No one spoke for a moment.

Then Bridget grinned slowly. "So… we missed something?"

Nia, breathless but smiling, propped herself up on her elbows. "Only the warm-up."

Lara flushed but didn't look away.

Tom stood very still — not shocked. Just moved.

Ella looked up, lips glistening with juices, and said simply: "This is how it started. And this is how it continues — with presence, with permission, and with no one left out… if they want to stay."

The candlelight danced on skin, and the door remained open — as it always had.

There was a beat — a breath — and then Bridget stepped forward.

She let her shawl fall from her shoulders in one fluid motion. Beneath it, she wore nothing. Her bush, copper-gold and proud, caught the candlelight.

She walked into the room like it was hers. "I was wondering when we'd get back to this."

Ella smiled up at her from between Nia's thighs. "There's room."

Bridget knelt beside Nia, kissed her softly on the mouth, then leaned forward to stroke Ella's back — slow, grounding touch, sensual without demand.

Lara entered next. Slower. Her eyes wide, but not afraid.

Tom didn't move at first — not out of fear, but deep respect. He watched Lara's hesitation, then slowly stepped behind her and kissed her bare shoulder.

"I've missed this," he whispered.

She turned to him, removed her blouse, and pressed her forehead to his.

Then she joined the others, folding herself down beside Nia, laying one hand on her thigh, the other on Ella's hip.

Tom undressed without drama. His body — already known, already welcomed — was met with soft glances and warm smiles.

The four of them now moved like one slow current — hands meeting hands, mouths finding skin, breath echoing off bare walls.

I watched them with awe. This wasn't group sex. This wasn't orgy.
This was **the Hedgerow** returning to its roots: shared pleasure as presence, shared skin as story.

Ella reached up from between Nia's legs and pulled me toward her. "Come back in."

I knelt, kissed her mouth, still wet with Nia's cum juices, then kissed Nia's mouth, where Ella still lingered.

Bridget lowered herself onto Tom's lap and guided him inside her with a long, low sigh. Her eyes locked on Lara, who reluctantly reached forward to kiss her lips and cradle her breasts.

And so the room moved — slowly, joyfully, without structure.
No one led.
No one followed.

Bodies touched and tangled and trembled, not to prove anything, not to impress, but simply to be.

At the centre of it all, Nia whispered once more:

"We never left the Hedgerow. We just let it bloom again."

And we did.

Together.

Lara hovered at the edge, naked, but still holding herself with quiet tension.

She watched the women — their mouths, their hands, the intimacy flowing between them — and admired it, even found it beautiful. But it didn't spark in her body the way it did in theirs.

Then her eyes fell on me.

I was kneeling between Ella and Nia, strong, centred, my cock half-hardened again, glistening faintly from Ella's kiss. And Lara's breath caught.

And then Tom — now standing just behind Bridget, fully erect, his size undeniable. He hadn't moved toward her yet, but his eyes were on her. Not with hunger — with invitation.

Lara felt a heat flood her thighs.

She stepped closer to me first, knelt before me, and placed a hand on my chest.

"I've missed this," she whispered. "Not the gathering. This. The sight of a man who isn't afraid to be open."

I cupped her cheek gently, our eyes meeting with mutual understanding. "Touch what you want. Nothing more."

Her hand drifted downward, slowly. When she wrapped her fingers around me, I exhaled — low and grateful.

Behind her, Tom stepped forward.

She turned, her eyes widening slightly as she looked at him. She bit her lip.

"I think," she said, breath unsteady, "I'd like to feel all of it."

Tom smiled, his hands warm on her waist as he knelt and kissed her belly.

And just like that, the Hedgerow folded Lara in — as she was. A woman who adored men. A woman who needed cock and muscle and the weight of a body moving inside her. And she was given exactly that — no shame, no compromise, no performance.

Bridget straddled Tom, her body moving in strong, circling rhythm, her hair loose around her shoulders. She bit her lip as his hands gripped her hips, guiding her onto him again and again. His cock filled her, stretched her, opened her.

Behind them, Lara was on her knees — I moved into her from behind now, steady and firm. She gasped with each thrust, her fingers tangled in the sheepskin rug. Her body sang with it — the fullness, the weight, the sheer rightness of it all.

Nia was lying on her back, Ella's fingers sliding in and out of her, slow and wet. One of Bridget's hands reached for Nia's breast, gently tugging her nipple until it peaked under her touch.

The room was all sound and skin — the slap of thighs, the glide of fingers, the squelch of juices, the rhythm of moans rising and falling like waves.

And then something began to happen.

It wasn't planned.
No one counted down.
But somehow, **we felt it** — a pull in the air, a shared tightening, a rising heat that synchronised across everybody.

Lara was the first.

Her whole body seized and shook as she came hard, me deep inside her, my hands holding her steady as she came again even harder — thighs slick, breath ragged, a soft 'fuck' slipping from her lips.

That tipped Ella.

She cried out into Nia's thigh, her fingers still stroking as her own climax rolled through her — slow, shaking, whole.

Then Bridget, grinding down onto Tom, threw her head back and gasped, "Yes… yes," as her orgasm took her — her walls clenching around him, soaking him.

Tom's control cracked a moment later. He groaned, loud and low, as he filled Bridget from beneath, his eyes locked on Nia's, wide with astonishment.

Then, still buried deep inside Lara, I came with a deep grunt — collapsing forward onto her back, my breath hot in her hair, my body pulsing against her hips.

And finally Nia — the last, the witness — came from the sound alone. The moans. The smells. The warmth. Her body trembled, wet and wide open, arms stretched above her head like she was offering herself to the night.

And then, silence.

Just breath.

Six bodies, trembling and tangled, bare and slick and glowing in the candlelight.

A room full of **completion**.

No guilt. No retreat. No confusion.

Only the soft truth of what had passed between us.

And Ella — voice hoarse, eyes shining — whispered:

"We are the Hedgerow. Not the idea. Not the myth. Just… this."

✦ ✦ ✦

Chapter 19
The Morning After

The sunlight came gently, peeking through the gauzy curtain like a whisper.

I stirred first. My arm was pinned beneath someone's hip — Ella's, I realised — but I didn't move. Her weight felt like an anchor in the best sense. Familiar. Honest.

The room was quiet, save for slow breathing and the occasional soft sigh as someone shifted in sleep.

Nia was curled on the rug, her legs draped across Lara's thighs. Bridget was still half-straddling Tom, their limbs wrapped as if they'd always been shaped to fit. Someone had placed a blanket over them in the night. No one remembered who.

I looked around at the five bodies — spent, glowing, open — and felt no shame. Just awe.

I eased my arm free and rose carefully, stepping over the scattered clothes and wine glasses. In the kitchen, I made tea — not to impress anyone, just because it felt like the thing to do. The kettle's bubbling didn't wake anyone. But the scent of mint and honey did.

Ella padded in first, hair wild, one breast marked faintly with teeth.

"You're a good man," she said, wrapping herself in a shawl and taking the mug I offered.

"No argument there," I murmured. "Think they'll all need one?"

Ella nodded toward the bedroom. "Some will need two."

Minutes later, one by one, the others appeared — yawning, stretching, moving like cats after a long sun nap. No one spoke about the night. No one needed to.

It was in the way Tom touched Bridget's waist as he passed her.
The way Lara glanced at me and smiled — small, but knowing.
The way Nia sat cross-legged on the floor, still bare, sipping tea like it was sacred.

We gathered at the kitchen table — the same table, I realised, where it had all begun.
Me, Ella, and Nia. Just a conversation back then. A longing.
And now, this.

I set down my mug and looked around the table. My voice was soft.

"This is how and where it all started. Nia, Ella, and me — at this kitchen table."

Nia smiled without lifting her gaze. "Back when we thought three was daring."

We laughed — quiet, real laughter — not from amusement, but from recognition.

Ella leaned her cheek on her fist. "Do we talk about it? Or just… sit in it?"

Bridget answered. "Maybe both. Maybe talking is sitting in it."

Tom chuckled. "As long as no one's expecting me to stand just yet."

That got a groan from Nia. "Please. If you stood now, we'd all be reminded."

Even Lara laughed. A full, open laugh — the kind that made her eyes sparkle.

And so we talked — not to analyse, not to dissect, but to remember. To honour. We spoke of hands and glances, of little noises, of what surprised them.

We didn't call it sacred.
We didn't need to.

It was.

By early afternoon, the flat had emptied.

They left in ones and twos — some with long hugs, others with quiet kisses, and a few with only a soft touch on the shoulder as they passed through the door. No one said goodbye. Just until next time.

I stayed.

Ella had insisted. "No one else gets to sweep up the candle wax. You're family."

So now I sat alone at the table. Just me. The original chair. The smell of lemon oil from someone's skin still faint in the air.

I picked up one of the glasses and turned it in my fingers.
A trace of lipstick curved along the rim. I smiled. I didn't
know whose.

The flat was still warm, despite the autumn outside.
Sunlight poured in — not fierce, just steady. Kind.

I looked at the kitchen where Ella had made tea that first
night.
Looked at the floor where Nia had stripped off her top,
almost absently, as if it had always been in the way.
I remembered the way she said 'I just want to be known,
like this'. And Ella nodding in silence.

We hadn't even touched that night. Not sexually. Just
undressed. Sat together. Breathed.

And now we were this.

I stood and crossed to the full-length mirror by the hall. I
looked at myself, at the body that had been held and seen
and welcomed. Lines on my hips. Slight softening at the
chest. A shadow of stubble on my jaw.

I didn't look younger. Just… real.

I thought about the word '**Hedgerow**.'

It had started as a joke, an offhand metaphor. Now it was
a living thing. A movement. A truth.

And yet, it still came back to that first night. To the three
of us. To the bare table. To that slow breath of 'yes.'
I exhaled.

I didn't know what was coming. I didn't know how long
it would last.

But I knew — without question — that I would follow
this path to its end.

And that whatever lay ahead, I would choose **meadow**
over **mower**. Every time.

✦ ✦ ✦

Chapter 20
Individual Confessions

Scene One: Nia

The bathroom was already full of steam by the time Bridget slipped in.

Nia was lying back in the tub, her legs stretched out, toes just peeking above the waterline. Her skin glowed with the heat, cheeks flushed, hair pinned loosely on top of her head with a few damp tendrils clinging to her neck.

"Didn't think anyone was up here," Bridget said softly, leaning against the doorframe.

Nia didn't open her eyes. "Didn't think I needed to announce myself."

Bridget smiled and stepped inside, easing down onto the wooden stool by the tub. The scent of something herbal — rosemary, maybe — floated in the air.

Nia finally opened one eye, then the other. "You can sit. But don't ask to share. I've earned this."

Bridget chuckled. "Wouldn't dream of interrupting."

A silence settled between them — not awkward, not even quiet. Just warm.

Bridget dipped her fingers in the water. "You always smell like pine and sex after a night like that."

Nia shrugged. "It's the real me. I don't do perfume."

Bridget watched a bead of water slide down the curve of Nia's thigh.

"You looked… free last night," she said.

Nia let her head rest on the back of the tub. "I was. I am. But it wasn't always like that."

Bridget glanced at her. "Want to talk?"

Nia laughed softly, not bitterly, just a little wry. "You ever try fitting into the queer scene as someone who still wants to be touched by men?"

Bridget blinked. "Isn't that… just being bi?"

"You'd think," Nia said. "But I was always told I was too soft. Too fluid. Not angry enough. Not loud enough. Like I needed a slogan to qualify."

Bridget was quiet.

"I remember this woman," Nia continued. "She had a buzzcut and Doc Martens and I was mad about her. I mean, properly dizzy for her. We kissed once. Just once. And then she said I 'didn't feel real'. That I didn't carry enough fight in me."

Bridget touched Nia's arm gently. "That's cruel."

Nia nodded. "I went home that night and shaved everything. All of it. Every inch. I stood in the mirror and told myself I'd grow it back just to spite her."

"And did you?"

Nia smiled slowly. "I did. That's when I knew who I was. Not angry. Not political. Just real. Just sensual."

She lifted one knee from the water and rested it on the edge of the tub, unapologetic, her soft mound lush with nature's own.

Bridget stared, not hiding it. "You're beautiful."

"I know," Nia said, not arrogant — just certain.

Bridget leaned forward. "May I touch you?"

Nia gave a small nod, her breath shallow now.

Bridget's fingers traced along Nia's thigh, then up, pausing just at the place where skin gave way to velvet. She didn't rush. Just explored. Reverent. Curious.

Nia's eyes fluttered shut again. "They said I didn't feel real," she murmured.

Bridget kissed the inside of her knee. "They were wrong."

And in the steam, with fingers and breath and nothing to prove, Nia let herself be fully seen.

Bridget's mouth hovered just above the damp skin of Nia's thigh.

"You know," she murmured, brushing a kiss upwards, "those lesbians you mentioned… they haven't got the faintest idea what they're missing."

Nia exhaled slowly, her eyes half-lidded. "Mmn. Say more."

Bridget smiled against her skin. "The softness. The scent. The heat. And this—" she slid her fingers into the folds of Nia's natural thatch, slow and appreciative, "—this gorgeous, untamed invitation."

Nia's head lolled to the side, her breath shallowing.

Bridget shifted her weight, placing one knee on the floor beside the tub, her other hand cupping the back of Nia's calf. "They thought they wanted edge. Anger. Posturing. But I'd choose this — you — every single time."

She lowered her mouth, kissing the edge of Nia's mound, not diving in but savouring it. Her tongue traced the edges, lingering, tasting the mix of rosemary water and something uniquely Nia.

A low hum left Nia's throat. "Keep talking."

Bridget kissed her again, then let her words drip between each flick of her tongue. "You're the kind of woman who blooms… slow. Who aches without asking. Who opens like warm fruit and makes you forget every damn argument you've ever had with your own body."

Nia's hand found the edge of the tub and gripped it. "Bridget…"

Bridget took her in now — tongue deep, inner finger teasing her clit, slow, rhythmic — but never hurried. One hand splayed across Nia's stomach, the other pressed gently against her inner thigh.

Nia trembled, not from nerves, but from the realisation that this moment — this woman — wasn't claiming her, correcting her, or trying to fit her into a shape. She was meeting her.

"I see you," Bridget whispered into the heat.

And Nia came — not with a scream or a gasp, but with a long, slow sigh that filled the room like incense. The kind of release that makes the body weightless for a while. Holy. Whole.

Bridget stayed close, resting her head on Nia's thigh as the aftershocks passed.

"I'm not political," Nia said after a long silence. "I'm just… hungry for honesty."

Bridget looked up at her. "Then you're in the right movement."

Scene Two: Tom

It was nearly dusk.

The garden behind Ella's flat was soft with gold, the sun slipping low over the tops of the fences. Birds called lazily from somewhere nearby, and the air smelled of cut grass and something warm — maybe from the neighbour's kitchen.

Tom sat on the old wooden bench, shirtless, feet bare, a beer in one hand. His skin still held the imprint of Bridget's nails from the night before.

Lara joined him without speaking, handing him a bowl of olives she'd found in the fridge. She wore a simple vest and boy shorts, her hair pulled up loosely. Her body was casual, relaxed — but there was always a sort of precision in how she moved, even when soft.

They sat in silence for a moment.

"Mind if I ask you something?" she said, popping an olive into her mouth.

Tom gave a small shrug. "Course not."

She looked at him directly. "Why does it matter to you? The bush, I mean."

Tom blinked, caught slightly off guard.

Lara went on. "I don't mean that in a challenging way. I'm just… genuinely curious."

He set his beer down, turning toward her slightly. "Honestly? I don't think it ever didn't matter. I never thought about it as some kind of preference. It was just… what I grew up loving. The first girl I was ever with had this gorgeous, dark triangle. I remember the smell of her — earthy and clean and real. I remember kissing her belly and pressing my face there like I was trying to remember what safety felt like."

Lara listened, eyes steady.

Tom scratched the back of his neck. "But over the years, every woman I got close to… they'd shave or wax, sometimes just because it was expected. One even apologised before undressing — like her body was something unhygienic."

He paused. "Made me feel like I was the one being weird."

Lara reached over and touched his thigh. "You're not weird, Tom. You're rare."

A silence stretched. Not awkward. Just thick with something unspoken.

"I've only ever told one other person this," he said, voice lower now. "When I wank, I imagine the hair. Not in some fetish way. Just… warmth. Realness. I picture parting it. Breathing her in. Feeling her move beneath me — not shaved smooth like a runway, but wild. Like I'm lost in something."

Lara swallowed. "Can I show you mine?"

He looked at her — really looked — and nodded.

She stood slowly and stepped out of her shorts, then peeled off her vest. Her breasts were soft and high, her stomach flat, and below, a golden auburn bush that glowed in the low light.

She stood still, letting him see.

Tom exhaled.

"It's beautiful," he said, almost graciously.

Lara stepped closer and straddled his lap, knees on either side of him on the bench. "Then show me how much."

He kissed her gently at first, then deeper, letting his hands explore her back, her thighs, her waist. His erection pressed up between them, obvious and unashamed.

She slid her hands into his curls. "You still think this is just comfort?"

Tom smiled against her collarbone. "It's home."

And there, in the hush of the garden, they moved together — not fast, not loud. Just limbs and breath and heat. As if he'd finally been allowed to worship something he'd never stopped believing in.

Scene Three: Bridget

The candlelight flickered low across Ella's lounge. A few bodies were still dozing on cushions or curled up under throws in the next room, but Ella had retreated here, nursing a small glass of port, one leg tucked beneath her on the old velvet armchair.

Bridget knocked softly on the frame and stepped inside.

"You still awake?" she asked.

Ella glanced up. "Barely. But just enough."

Bridget padded over and sat cross-legged on the rug near her feet. She was wearing a loose dressing gown, damp at the collar from a bath, and her hair was still tied in a knot on top of her head.

"I need to tell you something," she said quietly. "Something I never told anyone."

Ella sipped her drink and waited.

Bridget took a breath. "There was this man. This was years ago, when I was trying to be someone I wasn't. Trying to make myself fit. I fancied him. Really did. He liked me too — made that clear enough — but always with conditions."

Ella tilted her head slightly. "What kind?"

"He didn't like hair. Not anywhere. Said it reminded him of his mum, of the 'seventies' — made it sound disgusting."

Ella's face darkened slightly, but she said nothing.

Bridget continued. "So I did it. Booked the appointment. Lay down in some weird-smelling room with a woman I'd never met and had it all stripped. Every last strand."

She shivered slightly. "Afterwards, I stood in the mirror and didn't recognise myself. I looked… blank. Like someone had wiped something sacred away."

Ella reached forward and gently placed her hand over Bridget's.

"He still left," Bridget whispered. "Two weeks later. Said I wasn't 'playful' enough. Like I'd missed some secret performance he wanted."

Ella drew her hand up and stroked Bridget's cheek. "He wouldn't have known what to do with you even if you came wrapped in gold leaf."

Bridget let out a fragile laugh. "The worst part? I let it grow back in secret. Ashamed of wanting it. Every boyfriend after him, I'd shave before meeting them. Like I couldn't trust my own taste."

Ella shifted forward and opened the sash of Bridget's robe, slowly, gently.

"May I see you now?" she asked.

Bridget nodded, eyes glassy.

Ella eased the fabric aside, revealing the full, soft triangle beneath. It was thick, dark, and utterly natural — not styled, not shaped. It was what it was.

Ella smiled. "You're magnificent."

Bridget trembled.

Ella leaned in, lips brushing against the skin just above the patch. Then lower. She didn't rush. She kissed like someone reminding a sacred place it was still worthy of worship.

Bridget exhaled, then lay back, letting the robe fall away.

Ella's tongue traced slow circles, her hands firm against Bridget's thighs. And for once, Bridget didn't brace herself. She didn't perform. She simply received.

When the climax came, it was quiet — a soft quake of the stomach, a long sigh into her palm.

Ella lay beside her afterwards, arm over her waist.

"You never have to apologise for wanting to be seen."

Bridget turned her head. "I don't think I've ever really felt seen."

"You have now," Ella said softly.

Scene Four: Lara

The garden was still, damp with morning dew. A faint mist hung above the lawn like breath that hadn't quite settled. I stood near the apple tree, sipping black coffee from one of Ella's chipped mugs. The robe I wore clung slightly to my back, still damp from the shower.

Lara stepped out barefoot, pulling her cardigan tighter across her chest. Her hair was messy, her expression unreadable.

"I thought you'd be asleep," I said gently.

She shook her head. "Didn't want to be."

We stood quietly for a while.

"I had a dream," Lara said. "About being thirteen again. In the school changing rooms. I was the first girl to grow it — properly grow it. One of the others pointed and laughed. Said it looked like a squirrel had crawled into my pants."

I didn't laugh.

"I went home that night and cried," she continued. "My mum said it was beautiful. Said all women used to look like that."

I turned to her. "She was right."

Lara smiled faintly, her breath clouding in the cool air. "I kept it. Through the mocking. Through boys who'd touch me like I was alien. Through lovers who'd go down on me with confusion in their eyes."

She looked at me now, directly. "But not once did I ever want to be smooth."

I set my mug down on the low stone wall. "I'm glad."

Lara stepped closer. "You didn't look away last night. Not once."

"I never do," I said.

She opened the cardigan, slowly, deliberately. Beneath it, she wore nothing. The early sun caught the copper tones of her thick, natural mound — untrimmed, untamed, stunning.

I took a step forward, my breath catching. She reached down and guided my hand to her hip, then lower.

"You like this?" she whispered.

I nodded, my thumb stroking the warm curve of her.

"I used to think I'd never be wanted for it," she said. "Now, I don't want to be wanted without it."

I dropped to my knees on the damp grass without a word. Kissed the crease of her hip, the soft skin of her thigh, and then pressed my face against her, inhaling deeply.

Lara's hands tangled in my hair. "Slow," she whispered. "Take your time."

I did. Tongue and lips, mouth open and expectant, I tasted her like a secret I'd waited my whole life to learn.

She gasped, quiet but desperate, her hands tightening. The sun rose higher, warming her skin as she rocked gently against my mouth.

When she came, it was with a raw, low moan that disappeared into the morning mist.

I stood after, brushing the hair from her face.

Lara touched my chest. "That didn't feel like desire."

"What did it feel like?"

She kissed me, soft and lingering. "Belonging."

The sunlight had shifted again — softer now, angled through the blinds in golden stripes that lay across the rumpled bed.

Ella was resting against my chest, her legs entwined with mine, one hand lazily drawing circles on my stomach. Neither of us had spoken in a while.

Then, softly:

"I need to say something."

I looked down. "Go on."

Ella didn't lift her head. "I'm still gay."

I smiled gently. "I know."

She breathed in. "But I've never felt more… female than I do when you touch me. Not in a gendered way. Just… seen. Soft. Allowed."

I reached for her hand. "I didn't expect what happened either."

She finally looked up at me. "You're not confused?"

"Not even slightly," I said. "I think we just crossed into something that doesn't need defining."

Ella blinked slowly. "That makes it sound simple."

"It is simple," I said. "We care about each other. Deeply. We've shared something real. That doesn't rewrite your truth. It just expands it a little."

She rested her head back down. "When I was with women before, I always felt… understood. But never quite surrendered. With you, I felt like I could give in. Like I wasn't performing strength for anyone."

I kissed the crown of her head.

Ella whispered, "Maybe I've always needed both. Someone who understands my strength… and someone who lets me set it down."

I closed my eyes. "You did. And you still can."

We lay there in silence again, skin touching skin, no longer as lovers or labels — just as two people who knew the truth of each other's hearts.

Whatever we had between us now, it didn't need a name.

It only needed to be honoured.

Later, we sat side by side at the kitchen table. The same table where it all began.

Two mugs of tea steamed between us. Neither was in a rush to dress. Our bare skin had lost all performance — it was simply comfort now. Familiar. Honest.

I ran my fingers along a knot in the old wooden grain. "We were just talking, that day," I said. "Three of us. You, me, and Nia. Sharing stories. Laughing. That's all it was."

Ella nodded. "And then it wasn't. It became something… deeper. Something people needed, but didn't know how to ask for."

I looked over. "Do you remember what you said, right before we all got undressed for the first time?"

She smiled. "That if we can't face ourselves fully, we're only ever half alive."

I chuckled quietly. "It stuck with me. Still does."

Ella reached across and touched my wrist. "We were never trying to start a revolution," she said. "We just wanted to feel real again. In our skin. In our longing. In our difference."

I met her gaze. "And somehow, by doing that, we gave others permission."

A pause. Then Ella added, with quiet confidence, "I'm still gay, Simon. But if anyone ever asked me how I became fully me, I'd say it was because you let me come home to my body."

I swallowed. "You helped me do the same."

We leaned against one another in a warm, naked silence.

No shame. No confusion. Just shared breath, old wood beneath our thighs, and the simple knowledge that everything we had built — this messy, arousing, outrageous thing called

The Hedgerow — was born from nothing more than truth, trust, and the refusal to be trimmed.

✦ ✦ ✦

Chapter 21
The Return of the Ordinary World

Kate hadn't been to the market in months.

Not since her first visit to The Hedgerow.

She walked the familiar rows now — tomatoes stacked in wooden crates, basil in cellophane sleeves, the usual drizzle misting down from August clouds. Around her, voices rose and fell. Casual. Polite. Measured.

All of it felt oddly distant.

A woman bumped her shoulder gently at the fig stall. "Oh sorry, love."

Kate smiled reflexively, then watched the woman walk away — pressed jeans, handbag clutched high, waxed upper lip gleaming in the light. Everything about her was neat. Orderly. Stripped.

It struck Kate then: she hadn't worn underwear since the gathering. She could still feel the echo of wind against her skin, the weight of another body pressed into hers, the scent of rosemary and unshaved skin mingling in the warm dark of Ella's hallway.

Here, though, it was back to lip balm, restraint, and small talk.

She paid for her figs and moved on.

Later that evening, Kate sat on her sofa with a blanket over her knees and a cup of tea cooling beside her. She hadn't put the radio on. The silence suited her better now.

When her phone buzzed, she picked it up without looking.

Simon:

Just checking in. You alright?

She stared at the message. Her thumbs hovered, then finally tapped:

Kate:

Half alright. Half feral. Can I call you?

A moment later, they were speaking..

"Everything feels too quiet," Kate said.

"It's always like that at first," I replied. "After you've heard your real voice."

She pulled the blanket tighter. "I went to the market. It all felt… pruned. Airbrushed."

"You don't have to explain it to me."

"I know," she said. "That's why I called you."

We spoke for a while — about nothing, about everything. Then came a pause. The kind that holds a truth too big for either of them to name.

Finally, Kate whispered, "I don't want to lose this."

"You won't," I said. "It's in you now. You'll carry it wherever you go."

It started with a message.
Just after midnight.
Three words.

"You still up?"

Kate stared at the name. **David.**

An ex — not the worst kind, but certainly not the best.
They'd lasted four months.
He'd liked her laugh, her wit, her breasts.

But not her bush.

He'd never said it outright. Just a passing joke the second time they slept together — a comment about "keeping tidy." And a week later, she'd done it. Shaved herself bare. The silence between them after that was longer than any argument. A fortnight later, he stopped calling.

Now here he was. Two years gone. One message deep.

She waited five minutes before replying:

"Yes."

The second message came instantly:

"Wanna come over?"

Kate stared. Her first thought was no. Her second was, maybe. Her third — yes, but not for him.

She replied:
"Be there in 20."

David lived in a converted flat near the park. Same sofa. Same cologne.
Same shallow charm.

"You look… good," he said, eyeing her as she stepped in.

"I do," she agreed, unbuttoning her coat slowly. "Shall we skip the small talk?"

He grinned, clearly expecting a repeat of the past.
She walked ahead of him into the bedroom.

No lights. Just the soft blue from the streetlamp outside.

She pulled her jumper off, slid her leggings down.
He was already undressing behind her, the eagerness almost comical.

When she stepped out of her knickers, she turned — fully nude, hair wild, eyes calm.

And she watched it happen.

His eyes dropped to her hips. Paused. Flickered.
And then stalled — right there, at the thick, dark, magnificent triangle between her thighs.

He blinked.

She said nothing. Just stood tall and waited.

He cleared his throat. "You, uh… grew it back?"

Kate stepped forward, lips grazing his ear.

"No, David. I let it return."

She kissed him then — not tender, not aggressive. Just… dominant.

They fell into bed. She rode him slow. No moans. No
dirty talk. Just control. She kept her eyes open the entire
time. Watched him fall apart beneath her. He didn't dare
mention it again.

When she came, she didn't hide it. She gripped his chest,
arched her back, and let the sound fill the room.

Later, as he lay there, trying to gather his breath or his
pride, she dressed quickly.

"No need to text," she said casually, slipping her coat
back on. "This wasn't a reconnection. Just a reminder."

"Of what?" he asked, barely keeping up.

She turned at the door.

"That I never needed to be trimmed for you to want me.
And that now, I don't want *you* at all."

She left before he could reply.

The café hadn't changed.
Same flaky blue paint on the window frames, same
wobbly wooden tables, same smell of burnt toast and
cheap coffee.

Lara had only dropped in for a quick flat white. She didn't
even take off her scarf. But as she turned from the
counter — there he was.

Jamie.

The one who'd made her feel like a problem. Like hair was something to apologise for. Like her natural body was a conversation to be avoided.

They'd been nineteen.
It lasted six weeks.
He was smooth. Broad-shouldered. Polite to parents.
But in bed — hesitant. Guarded. Vague compliments, followed by awkward silences when his hand drifted too low.

She remembered it clearly now:
"Do you ever… do anything about that?" he'd asked one night, half-laughing, eyes averted.

She'd laughed back. Lightly. Too lightly.
And then cried in the shower.

That was the last time she let anyone make her feel unworthy in her own skin.

Now, here he was. Older. Still handsome, but softened by years of flattery and mirror-staring.

He looked up. Froze.

"Lara?"

She gave a slow smile. "Jamie."

They stood facing each other near the cream and sugar station.

"You look… amazing," he said, scanning her face. "Haven't seen you since—what, uni?"

Lara nodded. "Somewhere around the time you mistook confidence for defiance."

He blinked. "What?"

She tilted her head. "You always did have a talent for making things sound like compliments."

He chuckled nervously. "Look, I was young. Bit of a dick, probably. You were gorgeous, though. I just didn't get it back then."

"No," she said, lifting her coffee. "You didn't."

There was a long pause.

Then he lowered his voice. "Would you want to catch up sometime? Properly, I mean. You're still… just…"

She leaned in slightly — enough for him to smell her skin, the subtle scent of cedar and woman.

"You know," she said, voice low and steady, "I never changed. Not for you. Not for anyone."

Then, like it was nothing, she pulled back her coat — just slightly — and let him. see. The low-rise waistband. The soft dark edge of her wild, untouched self.

His eyes widened.

She smiled sweetly. "Still too much for you?"

Jamie opened his mouth, but no words came.

She turned, walking out with the confidence of someone who finally understood shame was never hers to carry.

The wine bar was quiet for a Friday.
Low jazz, dim lights, couples leaning too close.

Bridget spotted her straight away.

Marianne.

Her ex. Tall, sharp-boned, with that aloofness some
women wear like perfume.
They'd dated a year ago. Briefly. Intensely. Secretly.

Marianne had adored her — at first. The curve of her
body, the way she smelled in the morning, her laugh
when wine hit just right. But when things turned physical,
the compliments turned careful.

"It's just… you're a bit much down there."
**"I've never really been with someone who didn't…
you know."**

Bridget had trimmed for her once. Cried afterwards.
They broke up two weeks later.

Now, Marianne was across the bar, two fingers curled
around a glass of white.

Bridget walked past her intentionally, not to start anything
— but to be seen. Fully. Unapologetically.

Marianne looked up.

"Bridget?"

She turned, slow smile. "Didn't think you drank here."

"I don't. Not usually. You look… different."

"I am," Bridget said. "But only because I stopped
shrinking."

There was a pause. Marianne's eyes flicked downward — just briefly. The flash of skin between blouse and waistband. The edge of something dark and free.

"You seem well," Marianne said, voice tightening.

Bridget tilted her head. "I am. It's nice, being desired without editing myself."

Marianne gave a quiet laugh, brittle at the edges. "Still as blunt as ever."

"No," Bridget said gently. "Now I'm honest."

She took a step closer.

"You said once I made you feel wild. Like I was pulling you somewhere you weren't ready to go. And I believed that was my fault. I don't anymore."

"Bridget—"

"I'm not angry," she said. "Just clear."

She reached for Marianne's hand. Held it for a brief moment. Then pressed something into it — a folded card.

Marianne looked down. A sprig of heather was printed in the corner. No name. No contact. Just four words:

"The bush never lies."

Bridget turned and left.

This time, she didn't look back.

Chapter 22
The Line Between

It was Lara who brought her.

They arrived just before dusk — the golden hour slipping through the hedgerow like honey. The group had gathered in soft robes, cushions scattered in the grass, wine uncorked, bodies relaxed but bare beneath fabric. It was that in-between time: not yet naked, not yet formal, just present.

Lara held the woman's hand as they approached.

"This is Rowan," she said. "She's… one of us."

Rowan gave a quiet smile. Late thirties, maybe early forties. Curvy. Gentle face. Eyes full of admiration and something else too — nerves, tightly coiled and trying to stay hidden.

I stood and offered my hand. She took it with both of hers.

"I've read every word you posted," she said, voice low but sure. "I've wanted this for longer than I've known how to name it."

We made space for her on a blanket between Lara and Nia. Conversation flowed. Someone passed a bowl of grapes. The dusk deepened.

And still, Rowan's robe stayed closed.

Not one of us said anything.

Until she did.

"I feel like a fraud," she whispered. "I believe in this. Every part of it. I haven't shaved in years. I love my bush. I love what it means. But I just… I can't bring myself to—"

She glanced around. Everyone else was bare. Warm limbs resting on cool grass. Skin open. No shame.

"I'm not ashamed," she said quickly. "I'm not. But there's something… I don't know. Like I'm trying to cross this river and the bridge keeps shifting."

Ella leaned forward, voice soft.

"You're already here. That's the bridge."

Rowan nodded, eyes shining. "Lara told me what this place gave her. How it made her feel like she didn't need to apologise for her body. I want that. I want to stand up and just—" She stopped. Bit her lip. "But every time I think I'm ready, I freeze."

There was a long silence. Kind. Understanding. Not one face held judgment.

Then Nia, who'd once danced nude through a downpour to prove to herself she could, smiled and said gently:

"You don't have to strip to be seen. We already see you."

Rowan laughed, a little tearful. "That might be the sexiest thing anyone's ever said to me." We stayed that way for a while — no pressure, no coaxing, just presence. The Hedgerow wasn't a performance. It never had been.

But later, as the moon rose and laughter melted into quiet hums, Rowan did one small thing:

She opened her robe.
Not fully. Just enough.

Enough to let a soft triangle of dark hair peek through. Enough to let the night air kiss her inner thigh.

And no one stared.
They simply smiled.

Because in that moment, she had stepped into herself — and that, above all, was the point.

Rowan closed her robe in one swift motion, face flushed.

"I—I can't do this," she whispered, breath catching. "I thought I could. I thought I was ready…"

She stood suddenly, fingers fumbling at the tie, eyes shimmering with tears. "I'm sorry."

I rose without a word. Lara followed instantly.

"Come on," Lara said softly. "You don't have to explain anything out here."

I led them through the cottage and into the small back bedroom — the one with ivy brushing against the window and the quilt Ella had stitched by hand. The door closed quietly behind us.

Rowan sat at the edge of the bed, hands over her face.

"I feel like I've ruined it. Like I'm not worthy to be part of something so beautiful."

I knelt beside her. "This isn't a performance, Rowan. This is a practice. A belief. You're not failing — you're feeling."

Lara sat behind her, arms wrapped gently around her waist, resting her cheek against

Rowan's back.

And Rowan — finally — let herself cry.

It wasn't soft. It was heavy, wracking, unguarded.

"I was with someone once," she whispered between gasps. "A man who said I was wild in the beginning. Who used to moan when he went down on me. He said I smelled like something real. Said I made him feel animal. I loved that."

She breathed in, tried to steady herself.

"But then he changed. Said he couldn't take all the hair. That it made him gag. He told me he couldn't see me properly. That it was too much."

She looked down at her robe.

"So I shaved. And he left anyway."

Lara kissed the back of her shoulder. "You didn't deserve that."

Rowan nodded slowly, wiping her eyes. "Since then, I've grown it back. Every inch. But I've never let anyone see it. Not really. Not like this."

I stayed still, my presence quiet but unwavering. "Would you let us?" I asked gently. "Not to touch. Not to praise. Just… to witness."

Rowan hesitated. Then gave the faintest nod.

Lara slid off the bed and knelt beside me, both of us at her feet now — not as voyeurs, but as keepers of space.

Rowan exhaled.

She untied her robe again. Slowly. Carefully.

She let it fall open.

And there she was.

A thick, lush triangle of dark curls sat proud and soft between her thighs. Her belly rose and fell with nervous breath, but she didn't close her robe this time.

I looked up at her face, not her body.

"Beautiful," I said.

"Familiar," said Lara, eyes full.

Rowan's tears started again — but this time, they were softer. Calmer.

"I don't want to be scared of myself anymore," she whispered.

"You don't have to be," Lara said, rising to kiss her forehead. "Not here."

We sat like that for a long while — the three of us. No urgency. No arousal. Just truth.

Rowan's truth.

And when she finally stood — robe still loose, bush visible — she smiled.

"I'm ready to go back out."

The sliding doors opened gently.

Rowan stepped outside, the soft golden lamp-light from the cottage casting a glow behind her. She was barefoot, completely nude, her robe left folded on the bedroom chair.

She stood for a heartbeat.

And then she walked into the garden — naked, upright, radiant in the stillness.

The group turned. Smiles spread slowly. Then applause broke — warm, sincere, not performative. A wave of welcome.

Nia raised her glass. "To Rowan."

"To Rowan," they echoed.

Someone cleared a space. Ella offered her a cushion. Rowan sat, blushing but proud. Her skin flushed in the candlelight, her hair wild in the evening breeze, her bush, bold and beautiful. There was no shame left in her posture — just the quiet satisfaction of having crossed a threshold she never thought she'd find.

As conversation resumed and music trickled in from someone's playlist, Rowan settled in — at ease now, belly soft, legs folded, wine in hand.

But her eyes kept flicking to Tom.

He wasn't trying to be on display. He never did. But Tom's body, ever unbothered and natural, had a way of pulling the air around him. His legs were stretched out, head tilted back slightly, his cock hanging heavily between his thighs — thick, long, deeply unselfconscious.

Rowan tried to keep talking with Lara, but her gaze kept wandering.

Once. Then again.

And again.

Tom hadn't noticed at first. But Nia had.

She leaned closer to Rowan, smirking.

"Eyes up, love. Or don't."

Rowan gasped and covered her mouth, half-laughing, half-horrified.

"I'm not trying to stare!" she whispered.

"It's not a crime," Nia said, sipping her wine. "It's Tom."

Rowan shifted in her seat, clearly flustered. Her thighs pressed closer together, lips parting with a breath she didn't mean to let out.

Seated nearby, I caught the energy shift. My eyes met Lara's. She gave the faintest nod.

The evening began to tilt.

Tom finally glanced over, noticing Rowan's flustered glances — and her attempt not to look.

He smiled. Not cocky. Just open.

"You okay?" he asked, voice warm.

Rowan nodded, her voice caught in her throat. "Yes. Very."

Silence, then murmurs. The group sensed it — that edge of tension, the flicker of heat.

Tom didn't move. Didn't pose. But he let himself be seen.

His cock slowly began to rise — not in boast, but in response. Heavy, thick, hardening in the evening air, until it stood bold and strong, gently bobbing with his breath.

Rowan stared now, openly. Her hand drifted to her thigh.

And no one stopped her.

Because she was home.

And her desire — long buried, long stifled — had finally come alive.

The garden breathed with warmth.

Rowan sat quietly for a moment longer, watching the curve of Tom's erection rise in response to her gaze. Her hand lingered near her inner thigh, breath shallow, her lips parted.

But it wasn't just Tom she was seeing anymore.

It was Ella's bare hip brushing against Nia's as they whispered.

It was Bridget's fingers slowly tracing Lara's back.

It was the soft, familiar sound of a moan — not loud, not performative, just real.

The energy rose, slow and rich, like mist from warm earth after a summer storm.

Rowan stood.

No robe. No hesitation.

She stepped from the circle and walked toward Tom. Then paused.

"I don't know how to do this," she said, her voice raw but certain.

Tom stood too. "You don't have to.. do. Just… be."

She reached out and touched him — just his chest at first. Then lower. Her hand wrapped around his shaft, slow and reverent, as though touching something sacred.

He let out a low breath.

Rowan smiled.

Behind them, Ella had slipped behind Nia, her hands now roaming freely. Nia leaned into it, her own fingers trailing across Bridget's waist.

Lara had sunk to her knees beside me, gently stroking my thigh.

And Rowan — finally Rowan — let go.

She knelt beside Tom, taking him into her mouth, slow and sensual, not rushed, not frantic. Just willing. Just hungry in the way only true acceptance can allow.

Bridget moaned. Lara kissed Ella. Nia let her hand slide down my stomach until it found what it was seeking.

It was no longer about watching Rowan — it was about becoming with her.

Bodies folded into bodies.

Hands found hips, lips, nipples, mouths.

The Hedgerow moved together — not in pairs, not in performance — but in shared rhythm, shared breath, shared fire.

Rowan found herself lifted by hands, guided into arms, surrounded by warmth and skin and softness. She was kissed, licked, filled. She gave. She received. She opened.

She became one of us.

When it came — the wave, the ripple, the shared climax — it was collective. Breath caught, moans rose like birds from trees, and Rowan, at the centre of it, cried out.

Not from shame.

Not from fear.

From arrival.

From…. home.

Chapter 23
The Still Hours

The cottage had fallen into silence. Bodies rested, tangled and warm on blankets and cushions. The lanterns had burned low, casting soft amber glows along the timber walls. Outside, the garden crickets chirped like they always did after something beautiful.

Rowan stirred.

She rose slowly, quietly stepping over limbs and discarded glasses. The kitchen beckoned with the soft promise of water and solitude. Her bare feet made no sound on the wood floor.

She pushed the kitchen door open — .

I was already standing by the counter, a glass in hand.

I was naked too.

Our eyes met. We smiled. But there was something else in my expression — not quite shame, but self-consciousness. My hand subtly shifted, covering myself.

Rowan tilted her head. "You alright?"

I shrugged. "Didn't expect company."

She walked to the sink and poured a glass. "Thirsty."

A silence passed.

I looked down. "Bit silly really. Just… I saw your eyes tonight. With Tom."

Rowan blinked. "What do you mean?"

"I saw how you looked at him. At his cock." I chuckled softly, awkwardly. "It's alright. I mean — it's Tom. It's hard not to stare."

Rowan stepped closer. "Simon…"

I wouldn't meet her eyes. "It's not that I'm ashamed of mine. I just… saw something in your face I've never had directed at me. That wonder."

Rowan placed her hand gently on my forearm.

She spoke slowly. "It wasn't about his size, Simon. It was about the moment. The freedom. The fact I was finally allowed to feel that way, in public, without hiding."

She paused. "But you — you're the reason I got there."

I looked up.

"You sat beside me in that room. You asked to witness me. Not to use me, not to test me — just to see me. And that… that changed everything."

My throat worked with a swallow.

Rowan reached down gently, moving my hand aside.

She saw me now — soft, natural, unguarded.

"No comparisons," she whispered. "No need to measure."

And then she knelt.

Not to worship. Not to perform.

To reassure.

To honour.

She took me in her mouth with slow care, not needing me hard, not needing me eager — just present. Her hands held my hips. Her tongue moved with adoration.

I gasped — not from arousal, but emotion.

She stayed there until I stiffened gently, not fully, but enough.

She pulled back, kissed the head, and looked up at me.

"I meant what I said," she whispered. "You're the reason I got here."

Then she replaced her mouth over my cock, now full erection and pleasured until I came in her mouth.

I crouched down, kissed her forehead, and pulled her into a warm embrace. We stayed like that, tangled on the kitchen floor, the night humming softly around us.

We returned quietly, stepping barefoot into the warm hush of the sleeping room.

The air was thick with the scent of skin and sex and candlewax. Someone shifted beneath a throw; someone else exhaled softly in a dream.

We padded toward our space — a wide patch of sheepskins near the open doors.

And then we heard it.

A soft, wet sound.

A moan.

I turned. Rowan stilled.

There, lit faintly by a candle's final flicker, was Ella. On her back. Legs open. One arm tucked behind her head, the other between her thighs.

Her eyes were closed. Her hand moved in smooth, confident rhythm. Two fingers deep inside, slow and firm, her thumb circling her clit gently.

She wasn't performing.

She wasn't hiding.

She was simply being.

Her mound was full and natural, glistening, her breath catching slightly as her pleasure built in gentle waves.

Rowan didn't speak. I didn't flinch.

We paused only to witness. To admire. To respect.

Because this — this freedom, this comfort — was the Hedgerow.

Ella arched her back slightly, her hips lifting into her hand. A small gasp left her lips, followed by a satisfied sigh. She didn't even know we were there. She didn't need to.

Rowan smiled, a slow warmth blooming in her chest.

I gently lay down beside her.

We didn't reach out.

We didn't interrupt.

We just watched — for a moment longer — and let the hush of human pleasure lull us back to stillness.

As Ella came quietly into the early morning light, the Hedgerow held her, soft and silent.

Alive.

Chapter 24
Before She Leaves

The light had shifted.

Morning filtered through gauzy curtains, soft as breath, golden as honey.

Rowan stretched, the warmth of my arm still resting loosely across her waist. Around her, the Hedgerow began to stir — sleepy movements, skin against skin, small sighs of contentment.

She turned her head.

Ella had curled beside Bridget now, both naked and tangled like wildflowers grown too close. Nia lay half across Tom's chest, his arm casually cupped around her hip. Lara dozed on her side, her full bush resting like a shadow between bent knees.

Rowan exhaled.

It wasn't nerves this time. It wasn't fear.

It was hunger.

But not for food.

Not for validation.

For touch. For texture. For scent. For bush.

She sat up slowly, letting the blanket slip from her body. Her breasts swayed gently in the morning light. She didn't cover them.

Her thighs were damp with sleep and memories. Between them, she felt a slow, pulsing ache.

She rose.

Quietly.

I stirred, blinked. "You alright?"

Rowan turned, smiling. "Yes. I just… need a little more before I go."

I didn't question her. I simply nodded, my eyes soft.

Rowan stepped over Ella and Bridget, pausing for just a moment. She bent, kissed Ella's shoulder — then let her fingers gently stroke the soft mound nestled between Bridget's thighs.

Bridget murmured in her sleep, shifting slightly.

Rowan moved on.

To Nia.

To Lara.

To each of them.

She kissed.

She stroked.

She tasted.

With admiration.

With curiosity.

With a rising, unstoppable desire.

Each woman, now slowly waking, welcomed her without question — some with parted legs, some with soft sounds of approval. Some kissed her back. Others simply held her face and let her worship.

Tom, still half-asleep, opened his eyes and watched in awe as Rowan dipped between Nia's thighs and buried her tongue deep in the soft curls, moaning as though this act alone had been waiting in her forever.

I watched too, now sitting up, my cock slowly hardening again — not with jealousy, but with quiet reverence.

Rowan moved through them like nectar through petals, tasting each bush like it was a rare wine — no two the same, all equally sacred.

It wasn't about orgasm.

It wasn't about being seen.

It was experience. Full-bodied, earthy, female.

And when she finally collapsed back down beside me, breathless, glowing, her thighs slick with their essence, she whispered:

"I never knew what I was missing."

I kissed her, soft and slow. "Now you do."

She smiled against my lips. "And I'll be back."

Upstairs, the en suite door clicked quietly shut.

The water was already running, steam curling up the mirror, softening the edges of the world. Rowan stepped into the shower first, letting the warmth cascade down her body, washing away the remnants of the night — but not its meaning.

Behind her, the door opened again.

Ella entered without a word.

They didn't speak.

No need.

Ella stepped in, joining her beneath the stream. Her short hair darkened instantly, clinging to her jaw. Her body glistened, her bush dark and proud, pressed close as she reached for the soap.

Their eyes met.

Ella held the soap out. Rowan took it. Their hands touched — nothing dramatic, just wet fingers slipping against one another, lingering a second too long.

Rowan smiled. "I didn't know you'd be up."

Ella shrugged, stepping closer. "Felt you missing."

They were almost touching now.

Water slid between them.

"I'll be leaving soon," Rowan said quietly.

"I know."

The air between them was heavy with heat, not just from the steam. Rowan's gaze dropped — Ella's breasts were small, soft, the nipples just beginning to harden from the cool air beyond the water's reach.

"I've never…" Rowan began, then stopped.

Ella reached out and tucked Rowan's damp hair behind her ear. "You don't need to explain."

She leaned in.

Their lips met, gentle and curious at first — but it deepened. Not performance, not exploration. Connection.

Rowan's hands moved to Ella's waist, and Ella responded, letting the moment bloom between them. The water masked their soft sighs, their moans, the wet slide of mouth on neck, breast, thigh.

Ella turned slightly, guiding Rowan against the wall. Her hands ran down Rowan's back, then lower, parting her with a touch that was confident and slow.

Rowan gasped — her hips responding instinctively, her thighs trembling as Ella pressed closer, a finger sliding inside her, then another.

Their mouths never parted long. The steam clung to their skin, curling in the air like breath.

When Rowan came — her legs shaking, her voice caught in Ella's mouth — she reached for Ella in return. She dropped to her knees on the warm tiles and kissed the soft swell of Ella's bush as though it were sacred.

Ella looked down, eyes wide with pleasure and devotion.

Rowan worshipped her slowly. Her tongue moved with care and want, her hands steady. Ella moaned softly, her head tipping back, her fingers gently threading into Rowan's hair as the water rained down around them.

They stayed there a while, not rushing, not speaking — just moving, tasting, giving.

And when it was done, and they stood again face to face, Ella cupped Rowan's face and whispered:

"You belong here."

Rowan kissed her again, soft and final.

"Thank you," she breathed. "I know."

Chapter 25
The Note

The key turned in the lock with a familiar click.

I pushed the door open and stepped into stillness.

My flat smelled faintly of cedar and chamomile — a candle long forgotten. Dust danced in the light from the single window, undisturbed in my absence. Everything was where I'd left it. Everything, except the small white rectangle resting on the floor, just inside the door.

A note.

Folded. Neat.

No stamp. No envelope.

It had been slid under the door.

I paused — a quiet awareness settling into my chest. I bent and picked it up, my fingers brushing the paper's edge.

Just my name, scrawled in handwriting I didn't recognise.

Simon.

I turned it over.

Unfolded it.

And read. *'I know your mantra, I know your ethos — but do you forgive?'*

I took a photo of the note and sent it to the others — just the founding circle. Ella, Nia, Bridget, Lara, and Tom.

No idea who dropped it. Was waiting when I got home. Curious to hear your thoughts.

The replies trickled in slowly.

Ella was first.

Odd. Do you recognise the handwriting?

I replied: *No.*

Then Nia.

Strange choice of words… "Do you forgive?" Forgive who? What for?

Bridget replied an hour later.

Something about it… it's familiar. Not the writing. The tone.

Tom: *Trying to stir something, whoever it is.*

And then Lara.

A pause.

Then: *I keep hearing her voice when I read it.*

No name. But they all knew who she meant.

Rose.

I reread the note once more, hearing it in her voice now — the way she used to couch barbs inside polite language, always a layer of drama beneath her restraint. Always circling morality, blame, identity.

I know your mantra, I know your ethos — but do you forgive?

Forgiveness. A loaded word. One she would use with power.

I exhaled.

I typed back: *Could be. Might not be. But we need to be ready if she wants something.*

Ella's reply was instant.

She already wanted something. Now she wants back in.

I set my phone down. The quiet tick of the kitchen clock was the only sound.

Then another message arrived — one he hadn't expected.

Kate.

Hi. Sorry to jump in late, just saw the thread. Hope it's okay to share a thought?

I replied: *Of course. Always.*

There was a pause.

Then her message came through in full.

I know I'm still new to all this. But… when I read the note, it didn't feel like someone angry. It felt like someone who thinks they've been wronged. Someone who's trying to get inside your heads by pretending they already are.

That tone — it's not asking for forgiveness. It's testing whether you feel guilty.

Another pause.

That's what manipulative people do when they've lost power.

The group chat went quiet.

Ella finally responded: *She's right.*

I smiled faintly. It was easy to forget how perceptive Kate could be — quiet, thoughtful, but sharp in all the right ways.

Bridget added: *I like her. Let's keep her close.*

I replied privately to Kate.

Thank you. That helped more than you know.

Kate's response was simple.

I'm here. And I believe in this.

We met the next evening at Ella's place.

The same kitchen table.

The same circle.

Me, Ella, Nia, Bridget, Lara, and Tom.

Kate hadn't been invited this time — not yet. This wasn't exclusion. It was containment. The original six needed to speak freely, to remember the first principles of The Hedgerow before involving anyone else.

The table was quieter than usual.

Cups of herbal tea. A bowl of olives no one touched. Soft music hummed in the background, ignored.

I laid the note in the centre like an offering.

No one touched it.

Nia tapped the rim of her mug. "It is her. Isn't it?"

Ella nodded, slow. "Even if it's not… it might as well be."

Bridget leaned forward, resting her forearms on the table. "She's been waiting. Watching. The moment the mood shifts, she wants to return."

"She won't ask," said Lara. "She'll make us feel we owe her."

Tom finally spoke. "So what do we do?"

They all looked at me.

I didn't answer immediately.

Then: "We stay ahead of it. We hold steady. We don't react with fear."

Bridget raised an eyebrow. "But do we respond?"

"No," I said. "Not yet. Not until we're sure."

Ella looked at me. "And if it is her?"

My voice was calm. "Then we remember who we are. And who we're not."

Silence again. Heavy. Solid.

Then Bridget broke it with a smile.

"Shall I open some wine?"

✦ ✦ ✦

Chapter 26
The Whispered Return

Rose lit a cigarette she didn't need.

The small flat smelled of stale incense and something metallic — not blood, but close. A scent that came from old radiator pipes and unopened windows.

She stood at the kitchen sink, blowing smoke through her nose, staring into nothing.

The letter had been delivered. Slid under the door, exactly as planned. No cameras. No witnesses.

She hadn't signed it. That would have been too much. Too soon.

But the words?

They were perfect.

She'd read them back twenty, maybe thirty times before committing them to paper.

I know your mantra, I know your ethos — but do you forgive?

Let them chew on that.

Let them wonder.

Let them remember.

Because here was the truth — the part they couldn't see: she had been right.

She'd always spoken the truth. About the danger of self-indulgence. About the illusion of freedom in the

Hedgerow's sensual chaos. About how easy it was to manipulate desire if you knew the right words and wore the right skin.

They called her power-hungry.

They said she twisted the ethos.

But they never saw the whole picture. Not like she did.

Rose stubbed the cigarette out half-smoked.

There was movement behind her — the rustle of someone shifting in the next room. She didn't turn. Just said quietly:

"They'll come round. One of them will break first."

A voice replied. Smooth. Unplaceable. "And if they don't?"

She ran her finger along the sink edge. "Then we remind them… that nothing stays pure forever."

✦ ✦ ✦

Chapter 27
The Gate Is Closed

Rose arrived at the gathering uninvited.

Not at Ella's house, not the cottage — but a small community meet-up in town. A tea room the group sometimes used for low-key catch-ups with new members. Soft lighting. Mismatched chairs. A single candle on each table.

She walked in wearing black, hair tightly scraped back, a too-familiar smile on her face.

I saw her first. Then Ella. Then Nia, who almost rolled her eyes before catching herself.

Tom said nothing — he simply stood up and placed his chair in front of one of the newer guests, creating a quiet barrier.

Rose stopped.

The room had stilled. Even the kettle behind the counter had fallen silent, as if the air itself refused to move.

I stepped forward. Calm. Certain.

"Rose."

She nodded. "Simon."

"I got your note."

"I assumed."

I didn't ask why she was here. I didn't need to.

I simply said, "You're not coming back."

A pause.

"You don't forgive me?"

I glanced at the others. "We forgave you a long time ago. But that's not the same as inviting you back in."

Ella stood now. "You had your chance. You shaped something else. This… this isn't about blame. It's about resonance."

Rose opened her mouth — but Nia gently cut in.

"The bush never lies. You forgot that."

Rose hesitated. Her composure faltered for a flicker. Then she nodded — a sharp little movement, chin tilted higher than needed.

"I understand."

She left without another word.

Outside, the rain had just started.

Inside, a collective breath was released.

I turned back to the group.

"Tea?"

They laughed — not because it was funny, but because it was finished.

Truly, finally finished.

The parcel arrived two days after Rose's quiet dismissal.

No return address. Just Simon's name, scrawled in red marker.

Inside: a plain black USB stick, and a folded piece of paper.

Three words.

"You will never win."

I plugged it in, heart already hardening.

The video was crudely edited — a series of clips stitched together. Short scenes of women, filmed in bathrooms, bedrooms, changing rooms. Each one silent, mechanical. A pair of scissors. A buzzing razor. A growing pile of discarded hair. Some looked bored. Some looked defiant.

None looked free.

Rose's face appeared at the end, staring directly into the camera.

"If your bush is a symbol," she said, "then symbols can be erased. Rewritten. Rebranded."

The screen cut to black.

I sat still.

It wasn't erotic. It wasn't shocking.

It was sad.

Detached.

The opposite of everything *The Hedgerow* had become.

I reached for my phone and messaged Ella.

"She's still trying. But she's already lost."

We met later that evening — just the three of us.

Ella's place again. The same kitchen. The same table. The same silence that had, once upon a time, meant comfort.

I poured the tea.

Nia leaned back in her chair, arms folded, brow drawn. "How did it come to this?"

Ella spoke softly, "She wasn't always like that. I mean... she believed. In her own way."

I shook my head. "I'm not so sure. I think she liked the idea of us. Of freedom. Of being wanted. But when it meant honesty... skin... mess... she turned cold."

Nia snorted gently. "Cold? She's boiling with resentment now."

We fell quiet again.

Outside, the rain was still tapping softly at the windows.

Ella looked over at the USB on the counter. "Do you think she regrets it? Leaving us like that?"

"No," I said. "I think she regrets not being worshipped for the wrong reasons."

Nia took a sip of tea and stared at her cup. "It was never about praise. It was about being real."

I nodded. "And she couldn't stand being seen. Really seen."

Ella's voice softened. "We've all had moments like that. Nakedness can feel like judgement when you're not ready for it."

"But she was ready," said Nia. "Or at least she said she was."

"She was rehearsing," I replied. "Performing the idea of liberation without actually touching it."

Another pause.

Then Nia smiled faintly. "You know what she forgot?"

Me and Ella looked up.

Nia's eyes gleamed.

"The bush never lies."

Ella burst into a quiet laugh. I smiled, the tension easing a little.

I looked at the two women beside me. Their eyes. Their presence. Their naked souls.

"This is where it started," I said. "Right here. The three of us. Tea. Truth. No game. No rules. Just… real."

Ella reached for my hand. Nia reached for my other. And with one sharp movement my palms were cupping their bush. They both looked at me and said. 'We are here for this and everything it represents'

We sat like that for a moment. Warm. Present. Unshaken.

Ella's thumb traced lazy circles on the back of my hand. Nia leaned in just slightly, her arm brushing mine, the heat of her skin familiar and grounding.

No one spoke at first.

It was a slow return — not rushed, not dramatic. Just a shared breath between bodies that had always known one another.

Ella let go of my hand and stood. With quiet grace, she slipped her jumper over her head and let it fall to the floor. Her bra came next. She didn't perform. She didn't tease. She simply uncovered herself — as she had done that first time, when they thought this might just be a beautiful, passing idea.

Nia watched her, then turned to me. "Remember the first time she did that?"

"I do," I murmured.

"I wanted to cry," Ella said, smiling faintly. "Not from nerves — from relief. Like I didn't have to be anything else."

Nia reached up and unbuttoned her shirt. My eyes flicked from one to the other, breath deepening. The sensation wasn't lust alone. It was gratitude. That these women — bold, strange, brilliant — had chosen this. Had chosen me.

I stood and began to undress, slowly, methodically, like a ritual. Ella stepped closer, her hand pressing against my chest, sliding down, her fingers grazing my already rising erection.

"Still so easily moved by truth," she whispered.

Nia came up behind me, warm hands around my waist, her lips at my shoulder. "Let's forget her," she said softly. "Let's remember us."

Ella kissed me, slow and warm, while Nia pressed her bare breasts against my back, her hands roaming freely. The three of us moved in unison, like breath, like tide.

We brought each other to the floor, bodies twisting together like roots in soft earth. Ella's mouth found Nia's nipple while my fingers explored them both, careful and knowing. Nia moaned into Ella's mouth, her thigh pressed between my legs, grinding gently.

No words.

No roles.

Just heat and history.

I entered Nia as Ella kissed her, holding us both. Then Ella straddled me, guiding me inside her while Nia curled beside us, stroking, whispering, trembling.

When release came, it came in ripples — Ella shaking, Nia gasping, Me groaning low and deep. We collapsed together, skin damp, hair tangled, chests rising and falling in near-perfect rhythm.

After, we lay tangled on the rug, laughter slowly replacing breathlessness.

"We're still *The Hedgerow*," Nia whispered.

I smiled. "Always."

We lay quietly for a while, limbs draped, hearts steady.

Ella stretched, her fingers trailing over her own belly. A slow smile crossed her lips as she looked at me and Nia, still flushed and glowing beside her.

"You know I love watching," she said gently, her fingers wandering downward with ease. "I always have. It's how I first knew I was safe here… watching you both, seeing how honest it was."

I turned, amused. "You're insatiable."

"Mmm," Ella hummed. "But not greedy. I don't need to join. I just want to… feel it with my eyes."

Nia grinned. "That's the gayest thing you've ever said."

Ella laughed softly. "Then let me be gay and glorious. Show me what you've got."

I looked at Nia, who was already sliding onto my lap, her hair tumbling around her face. I reached for her, not just with hands but with intention — every touch a shared memory, every movement a silent promise. We kissed, deeply this time, like breathless language.

Ella's hand moved in slow, steady circles between her legs as she watched us move together. She bit her lower lip, not from shame but from sheer pleasure. Her fingers moved faster as me and Nia moaned, our rhythm building, Nia's breath growing sharp and shallow.

And when they came together again — Nia trembling in my arms, me groaning into her neck — Ella cried out softly too, hips rocking upward into her own palm, her legs shaking as her orgasm crested with theirs.

The three of us collapsed into silence once more, this time spent, this time still.

"We were always this," Ella said after a while. "Not performance. Not rebellion. Just… permission."

Nia nodded, her head on my shoulder. "To be naked. In every way."

✦ ✦ ✦

Chapter 28
The Space Between

The morning sun pushed gently through the curtains, casting a warm glow over tangled sheets and quiet limbs. The scent of sex still lingered, but it had softened — now just part of the atmosphere, like memory.

I stirred first, blinking slowly. Beside me, Nia lay awake, her eyes fixed on the ceiling, her fingers laced on her stomach.

"You're already thinking," I murmured.

She turned her head. "Mm. I am."

I waited.

She hesitated.

"I've been offered something," she said quietly. "A role. In Leeds."

I sat up slightly. "Leeds?"

She nodded. "Outreach. Community arts. They want me to head the whole programme. It's good work, Si. Proper work. The kind that helps people."

Ella padded into the room, naked, with three mugs of tea. "What's this about Leeds?"

Nia gave her a faint smile. "I'm moving. End of next month."

Ella paused, tea in hand. "You're serious."

"I have to go," Nia said, gently. "This… *Hedgerow*… it's changed me. It's freed me. But I need to give that back, somehow. In my way."

I looked down at my hands. "I thought we'd always be here. At least you would."

"I thought so too." Nia took a sip of tea, then looked at Ella. "And you?"

Ella sighed. "Funny you should ask. Brighton. The LGBTQ+ centre wants me to run their new wellness branch. I said maybe."

I laughed, but there was no joy in it. "So I'm the only one staying behind."

"No," Ella said. "You're the one staying rooted. Which might be the most powerful thing of all."

Nia added, "You're not being left, Si. You're being trusted — to keep this alive."

There was silence for a moment.

Then I looked between them. "So… is this the end?"

Ella sat beside him. "Not the end. Just the next season."

Nia leaned in, kissed me gently on the cheek. "Hedgerows don't die. They grow wild — in all directions."

In the weeks that followed, the rhythm shifted.

It wasn't spoken aloud, but everyone felt it — the tremble of change beneath the surface. Nia's move to Leeds. Ella leaning ever closer to Brighton. Two founding roots preparing to stretch into new soil.

But before they went, there was a need to gather. To hold the Hedgerow in their hands one last time as it had been, before it became something else entirely.

We sent word to Bridget, Lara, Kate, Tom, and Rowan — no big show, no formal gathering. Just a quiet invite, like the very first time: *Are you still in? Still with us?*

One by one, they came.

In my flat, in Ella's kitchen, even once at Rowan's countryside studio — we gathered. Shared food. Told truths. Took our clothes off slowly and without ceremony.

Each person was given a moment — not to justify, not to perform, but to reaffirm.

Bridget was first. "You know me. I don't believe in following things blindly. But this? This gave me myself back. I'm still in. As long as we stay real."

Tom, ever the quiet one, simply said, "I've never been more honest than I am here. Count me in."

Lara, with her arms folded but eyes soft, added, "I used to think I had to hide the parts that made men uncomfortable. Not anymore. I'm not going backwards."

Kate nodded. "I may not speak much in the group… but I feel more seen naked here than I do clothed anywhere else."

And Rowan, smiling now with ease, said, "You helped me shed more than my robe. I don't want to go back to hiding."

Each voice added strength to my resolve. I didn't have to lead alone — not really. What they had built was a network of trust, not a hierarchy. And as Nia and Ella prepared to leave, it wasn't an ending. It was a handing over.

The Final Bloom

We called it *The Final Bloom* — a farewell not to the Hedgerow itself, but to the time when they were all still here, together.

There would never be another night like this. Not with these people, in this space, still unchanged by distance, by dilution. This was the last true gathering of the original bloom. And they all knew it.

The room was ready.

Layers of rugs. Low lights. Bowls of summer fruits. Earthy scents from the diffuser — sandalwood, patchouli, something green. The windows were open just enough to let the night in. It smelled like warm leaves and dusk rain.

No one arrived fully clothed.

They had all agreed on that without a word. It was a ritual now — a way of saying: 'I trust you. I came honest.'

Bridget wore only a long silk scarf around her neck. Lara had a flower tucked into her hair. Kate, barefoot, painted her toenails dark green for the occasion. Rowan, glowing with recent confidence, came in a soft linen robe — but let it fall to the floor within moments.

Ella and Nia were radiant, skin bare and unashamed. I, for once, said nothing — my body already speaking everything I felt.

We gathered in a loose circle, soft music playing. Someone poured wine. Someone peeled an orange and passed the segments round.

There was no rush.

Tom sat behind Lara, hands on her waist. She leaned back into him, eyes closed. His fingers drifted down her belly, but there was no urgency — just slow, grounding presence. They kissed, deeply and fully, as if no one else were there.

Across the room, Rowan brushed Bridget's thigh with the backs of her fingers. Bridget leaned into her, and their mouths met, mouths familiar now — warm and eager. Rowan knelt between her legs, eyes locked with hers as her tongue began to work in slow, teasing circles. Bridget moaned and arched, one hand on Rowan's head, the other on her own breast.

I watched, breath quickening. I felt a shift beside me. Ella.

She reached for my hand and placed it on one breast. "I want to feel you again. One last time. Not for ownership. For memory."

I bent down and kissed her nipple — soft, tender — then lay her back. My fingers found her wet and open, and she gasped as I entered her slowly, deeply, Nia curling up beside us, her lips on Ella's shoulder as they moved together.

Nia joined next — straddling Ella's face as I thrust from below — and for a moment it was a perfect tangle: three bodies in rhythm, lips and tongues and hips all speaking the same wild, wordless language.

In another corner, Kate and Lara kissed for the first time. It was clumsy, surprising — a kind of joyful accident. They laughed into each other's mouths, their fingers wandering with curious hunger. Tom, watching, grew hard again, and this time Bridget crawled over to him, grinning.

"I've missed this cock," she said, her voice low and thick.

Tom groaned as she took him in her mouth, her hands cupping his balls, her tongue slow and precise. Behind her, Rowan kissed her spine — featherlight — until Bridget turned, pulling Rowan onto all fours beside her.

The group moved like a current — bodies joining, separating, recombining.

No jealousy.

No shame.

Just flow.

Ella lay against the cushions, watching the scene, one hand between her legs, smiling like someone watching a sunrise. "This," she whispered to herself, "is what the world is missing."

As climax after climax pulsed through the room — moans overlapping like waves — something unspoken passed between us. We knew this wasn't repeatable. Not like this. Not again.

But that was the beauty of it.

When the final shudders subsided, we lay together in a tangled heap — skin on skin, hair mingled, breath syncing slowly.

We didn't talk about where we were going.

We didn't talk about who we'd been with.

We didn't need to.

What mattered was this: the touch of a thigh, the weight of a hand, the sweat on a brow. The bush, in all its forms, was there in every scent and stroke — untamed, lush, proud.

It was Hedgerow.

And even when it scattered, it would root itself again.

✦ ✦ ✦

Chapter 29
The Doorbell

Autumn had settled in. The days grew shorter, and the air held that dry, brittle chill that

signaled the end of things. Trees shed their leaves with quiet grace. Life, too, had begun to slow.

It had been months since *The Final Bloom*. Nia was up north now, building something new. Ella had found a creative collective in Brighton, working in community arts and women's spaces. Messages were still exchanged. The occasional group thread pinged with a photo or a "miss you," but the meetups had grown thin. Scattered. Life, it seemed, was creeping back in.

I had returned to a quieter existence. My flat, once humming with visitors and spilled wine and naked laughter, now felt like a held breath. I still lit candles. Still left my bedroom door open. But the air was still.

Then — one Friday evening, as I stood in the kitchen spooning herbal tea into a pot — the doorbell rang.

Not a buzz.

A bell.

Sharp. Unmistakable.

I froze.

No one used the bell.

Not since... then.

I dried my hands and walked to the door, pulse steady but alert. The hallway was dim. The silence grew thick.

I opened it.

There she was.

"Kate," I said quietly. "Hi."

She stood with her coat clutched tightly at the front, cheeks pink, eyes uncertain. Her fringe stuck slightly to her forehead in the cool air.

"Can I come in?" she asked.

I stepped aside.

She walked in slowly, eyes scanning the flat as if revisiting something sacred.

"I wasn't sure you'd be in," she said, unbuttoning her coat but not removing it. "I almost didn't ring."

"You could've messaged," I replied, gently.

"I didn't know what to say."

She turned then — fully — and I saw it. The glisten in her eyes. The hesitation. The ache. It wasn't regret. Not quite. It was something older.

"What's happened?" I asked softly.

Kate smiled. "Nothing dramatic. No scandal. I just… I was walking home. Past that little bakery near the park — the one where we saw Rowan that day — and I remembered the way we all sat in your living room once, passing fruit around like it was treasure. Bridget had honey on her chin."

I chuckled.

Kate continued, her voice quieter now. "I missed that. Not just the sex — though god, the sex. But the freedom. The honesty. I miss being around people who don't want me to

apologise for… for being soft. Or messy. Or having a fucking bush."

I smiled. "You still do?"

Kate nodded. "Always."

A pause.

Then: "Do you?"

I looked at her for a long time, then slowly unbuttoned my shirt and peeled it off. Kate stepped closer. I placed her hand on my chest.

"I never left it," I whispered. "I've just been waiting."

Kate kissed me, gently at first. Then with heat. Her coat slipped to the floor.

Kate's coat pooled silently at her feet, and she stood before me in a simple black dress — the kind worn for comfort, not seduction. But on her, now, in this moment, it became both.

My fingers brushed the edge of the fabric where it hugged her hips.

"Are you sure?" I asked.

"I wouldn't be here if I wasn't." I guided her gently backwards, through the low-lit hallway, into the living room. The same living room where so many nights had passed — but now stripped of others, of crowd and chaos. Just two bodies. One moment.

Kate unzipped her dress slowly, letting it slip off her shoulders. No bra. No pretense. She stood, arms at her sides, fully present — the soft dark triangle at her centre full and proud.

I let out a quiet breath as I undressed in front of her. I was already hard, not from lust alone, but from recognition. The way her eyes stayed on me. No judgement. No comparison.

Just yes.

We laid down on the large blanket I'd never folded away. The same one we'd shared before. Familiar texture beneath us. Familiar warmth rising between us.

She moved first — straddling me slowly, skin against skin. Her hips rolled instinctively, and my hands found her waist. There was no rush. No choreography. Just breath and friction and the sound of her low moan as I slid inside her.

Her body welcomed me like a memory.

She leaned down, brushing her nose against mine. "You still smell like cedar."

I smiled, hands cupping her backside, guiding her rhythm.

She rode me slowly at first, her bush brushing my stomach with every tilt of her pelvis. I looked down, watching the way her body moved, how fully she gave herself to this — to me.

Her breasts bounced gently as her pace increased, and I raised my mouth to suck one nipple, then the other, my tongue circling, teasing, worshipping.

Kate arched.

Our rhythm deepened.

My hands slipped between her thighs, fingers finding her clit, stroking in time with her motion. Her eyes fluttered shut.

"I missed this," she gasped. "God, I missed you."

I whispered, "I never stopped thinking about you."

Kate's orgasm came like a wave breaking — sharp breath, clenched fists, full-body tremble. She cried out into my mouth, her body pulsing around me, and I held her tightly as I

followed, spilling my cum deep inside her with a groan that came from my chest.

We lay still, sweaty and tangled, her head on my shoulder.

Minutes passed.

"I needed that," Kate whispered.

"So did I."

She raised her head slightly, looking at me.

"Maybe this is how it comes back," she said. "Not in big parties or loud declarations. Just... one by one."

I nodded.

"The Hedgerow doesn't die," I murmured. "It just roots deeper."

Chapter 30
New Shoots

It began again with a voice message from Ella.

I was in the bath — a long soak, eucalyptus salts, candle flickering on the tiled ledge — when my phone buzzed on the floor nearby. I ignored it at first, eyes half-closed, steam curling lazily around the room. But the tone caught my attention. Ella rarely sent voice notes.

I leaned over, dripping, and pressed play.

"Hey, you. Just wanted to share something odd — but good-odd. There's this girl I've met here through the arts space. Fiery, funny, full bush and not shy about it. We ended up chatting after a community drawing session… and Simon, she knows. Not about us, not the name or anything… but she gets it.

She continued, *'I'm tired of apologising for my body. I want to be seen, not shaved.'*

I didn't even flinch. I just… smiled. And I told her: there's a place where that feeling lives.

She wants to hear more. I'll be careful. But I think the Hedgerow is growing here. Quietly. Naturally. Like moss on stone."

I smiled.

A few days later, another message came through.

This time from Nia.

Text only, short and sharp — her style to the letter:

"Two women. A rooftop gathering. Candles, wine, no shame. They brought up body hair in front of six men and didn't blink.

I said nothing. Just listened. But the seed's there. I think… I think it's sprouting."

I stood by the window, phone in hand, watching a flock of starlings twist in the sky like

ribbon.

For the first time in months, I didn't feel like I was missing something.

The Hedgerow hadn't ended.

It had scattered.

And now… it was blooming again. In corners. In hearts. In whispered confessions over wine. In touch. In truth.

The movement we'd started was no longer ours alone.

It belonged to the world now.

✦ ✦ ✦

Chapter 31

The Last Meadow

The end of the beginning.

It wasn't a party.
Not like before.
No banners. No plan. No pressure.

Just a message.

A simple, quiet message from me to each of them:

One last walk. No rules. Just us. The meadow. Bring nothing. Wear less.

And so they came.

Lara, first. Then Tom.
Bridget arrived in silence, her curls looser than usual.
Kate brought a warm flask of something herbal and comforting.
Rowan came barefoot, her robe forgotten, her face serene.

We met at the field beyond the bend — where the long grasses swayed and summer still lingered, thick and golden.

There was one person missing.

Ella.

She had written to me. A handwritten letter, folded three times and scented faintly with lavender.

"I can't be there, love. Not this time. But my body remembers. My skin remembers. What we built… it's in me. Always will be. Sit where we sat. Touch where we touched. And if there's still warmth in that patch of grass, that's me — holding space. Wild and watching."

So we left a space open in the circle. No one lay there. No one spoke. But the presence was felt like breath on bare shoulders.

We undressed as the sun softened — quietly, without show. A button here. A hem there. Then hips, thighs, curls revealed like secrets finally safe to be seen.

No commentary. No giggles.

Just reverence.

The bush — unashamed, varied, natural — was everywhere. And in the stillness of the

moment, it felt like a prayer.

We lay in the meadow — skin on earth, hand in hand, remembering.

I looked to the place where Ella might have lain. "It began here," I whispered. "In trust. In body. In bare truth."

Kate nodded. "And it ends here. Not broken. Just… open."

Tom raised the flask lazily, his voice low: "To Ella. And to all of us."

A soft murmur of assent.
Then the words — spoken without prompt, as if the land itself requested it:

"To Nia, The bush never lies."

A kiss followed. Then another.
Then breath, then skin, then the aching closeness of bodies reuniting — not for spectacle, but for meaning.

We moved together. Not wildly. Not desperately.
But with clarity. With memory.
With a kind of sacred joy.

Our final climax came like the setting sun — slow, glowing, inevitable.

When it passed, we lay in a tangle, the air cooling around us, dusk folding in like a soft

 curtain.

I turned my head, eyes half-lidded. "This… was never just about sex," I said quietly.

"No," Bridget replied, running fingers through the grass. "It was about returning."

We stayed until the stars were visible — quiet, breathing, together.

Ella never arrived. But in that quiet space we left, no one doubted she was there.

✦ ✦ ✦

Epilogue

They didn't just take the hair.
They took the heat, the scent, the wildness.
They took the part of womanhood that wasn't polite.

They told them it was ugly.
Unclean.
Unwanted.

So they shaved it off — to be wanted.
They waxed it smooth — to be accepted.
They learned to hate what made them real.

But they lied.
Because the bush was never the problem.
The problem was power. Power is quiet when women
disappear themselves.
When they apologise for their scent.
When they try to make their bodies smaller, cleaner,
softer.

But some of them stopped saying sorry.
Some of them let it grow. And what came back wasn't
just hair.
It was fury.
It was memory.
It was sex.

And it won't be taken again.

The End

The Hedgerow